Adventure Stories for Daring Girls

Retold by
Samantha Newman

Illustrated by
Khoa Le

ARCTURUS

This edition published in 2021 by Arcturus Publishing Limited
26/27 Bickels Yard, 151–153 Bermondsey Street,
London SE1 3HA

Author: Samantha Newman
Illustrator: Khoa Le
Editor: Donna Gregory
Designer: Ms Mousepenny

ISBN: 978-1-83857-985-2
CH007799NT
Supplier 29, Date 0721, Print run 11178

Printed in China

CONTENTS

Introduction

Dear reader, do you like adventures? You do? Oh, good. Because the book you are holding is absolutely crammed full, bursting at the seams with ADVENTURES. Lots of people think that an adventure is something you have to go far, far away to experience—that you have to trudge through a wilderness, climb a mountain, defeat a bad guy, and escape death at least once before breakfast. But the truth is that an adventure can happen anywhere, if you know how to have one.

So, here is a handy guide to having an adventure:

1. FIND YOUR MISSION

Have you spotted someone who needs your help? Or is there a new place you want to explore? Or perhaps an important object you want to retrieve? Maybe you've got lost and need to find your way home? Congratulations, you've just found your mission and you are ready for Step Two.

2. TAKE THE FIRST STEP

This sounds easy. It's just lifting your foot up and putting it down again, after all! But the first step is the most important—and the most difficult. If you've chosen to have your adventure, you might be ready to bound out of the door with a pack full of provisions. But otherwise, it might take a lot of bravery to begin. Which brings us onto Step Three …

3. FIND YOUR BRAVERY

Everyone knows that you must be brave to have an adventure. But not everyone knows that we all have a bit of bravery inside of us. That's right, absolutely everyone! And there is nothing like an adventure to bring out your courage, whether it's needed to stand up to bullies, to fight a terrifying monster, or to travel somewhere new. Being brave doesn't mean you never get afraid. It means that you carry on even when you are afraid!

The girls in these stories are from different places all over the world. Their lives and situations are diverse, but they all have the heart and determination to stand up for what's right—for themselves and others.

So, are you ready to battle a Snow Queen with loyal young Gerda? How about a journey from space alongside curious Princess Kaguya? Or perhaps you would rather fight an invading army alongside fierce Hua Mulan? This book will take you from an Alpine village, across the deep ocean, through the topsy-turvy world of Wonderland, up through the sky to Oz, and then spin you back through the forests of Russia and many other fantastic places besides.

Grab any provisions you need. (All adventures require a snack or two!) Next, find yourself somewhere comfortable and quiet. (Being interrupted is no good for adventures.) Now, it's time to become friends with these wonderful, intrepid girls. Live their stories with them and hold them close. Then, maybe one day, you will be ready to have a thrilling adventure of your own.

Gerda and the Snow Queen

Adapted from *The Snow Queen* by Hans Christian Andersen

Gerda and Kai were the very best of friends. They lived next door to each other in a town in Denmark. Their bedroom windows were opposite each other, and so close that they could visit each other by climbing straight across. They loved to play in their window-box gardens. Together, they had grown several beautiful red roses. They would even hear their bedtime stories together. One snowy night, they were snuggled down, watching huge snowflakes fall outside. Kai's grandmother was telling them a story. She told them that sometimes, the snowflakes weren't just snowflakes. Sometimes they were Snow Bees.

Just like all other bees, Snow Bees had a queen. She looked like a human queen, crowned with ice. She ruled the snowy winters. Kai's grandmother said if they looked where the snowflakes clustered the most, they would find the Snow Queen.

The next day, Kai and Gerda played in the snow, as usual. They took their sleds down to the town square and waited for passing sleighs to hook them onto, so that they could have a fast ride along the road. It was great fun! At dusk, they knew it was time to

go home. But while Gerda went straight indoors for some of her grandfather's delicious hot cocoa, Kai pretended he was going inside, but then crept back to the square.

Just one more ride and then I'll go home, he promised himself.

The town square was empty now, lit only by the moon and the street lanterns. It was so quiet, Kai was about to give up and go home when a pair of great white polar bears came whizzing into the square in a flurry of snowflakes, pulling a big white sleigh driven by a lady in a white fur coat.

Kai couldn't believe his luck as he hooked his sled on. The sleigh was so fast and it was a thrilling ride through the slippery streets. Before Kai knew it, they were outside the town and the sleigh stopped.

The lady's face appeared over the side of the sleigh, surrounded by floating snowflakes. She was very beautiful and wearing a crown of golden shards. "Did you enjoy your ride?" she asked. Her voice sounded exactly like the tinkling of icicles falling off a roof.

Kai nodded. The lady smiled. It was the coldest smile Kai had ever seen—but also the most beautiful. "Do you know who I am?"

Kai suddenly remembered the description from Grandmother's story and fear gripped his heart. "You're—you're the Snow Queen!" he gasped.

Her smile widened, like a crack opening in a frozen lake and the Snow Bees buzzed around her. "That's right."

The Snow Queen kissed Kai once on the forehead so he would not feel the cold. Then she kissed him again so that he forgot about his family and friends. Kai took her hand and climbed into the sleigh. Away they rode, leaving Kai's home, and all those who knew and loved him, far behind.

The next morning, Gerda woke to the news that Kai was missing. She raced outside to look for him in all their usual spots, but Kai was nowhere to be found. As she passed the nearby river, a little boat floated toward her, stopping right by her on the bank.

Gerda gasped. "Mr. River, do you know where Kai is?"

The river gurgled and bubbled and the boat bumped the bank again, so Gerda climbed in. "Please take me to him!"

The river carried her far and fast, through small towns and big cities and dense forest and snowy hills. She could not steer the boat to the side of the river to stop. Soon Gerda was farther away from home than she had ever been. After sailing for nearly a whole day, the boat gently pulled over in the most peculiar spot. The bank it bumped up against this time was not covered in snow, but lush, green grass. As Gerda stepped out of the boat, she felt warm sunshine beating down on her head.

She found herself in the garden of the Sorceress of Summer. It was the most beautiful, bloom-filled paradise and the Sorceress herself was a friendly, twinkly, older lady, dressed in flowers from head to toe.

She welcomed Gerda warmly and offered her food and drink. As Gerda went into the Sorceress's cottage, she paused to admire a bush of red roses.

"These remind me of my best friend, Kai," Gerda said. "I'm actually here to look for him—have you seen him?"

"I'm afraid not," said the Sorceress.

As Gerda skipped inside, the Sorceress waved her hands and every rose bush in the garden sank beneath the ground. The Sorceress was very lonely and now that Gerda was here, she didn't want her to leave. In the house, she fed Gerda delicious treats, all filled with a small amount of Forgetfulness Potion, so as Gerda ate, she soon forgot her family, her town, and Kai. She thought she had always lived with the Sorceress.

Gerda stayed for a very long time, playing in the sunshine for days on end. Then, one day she saw a red rose on the Sorceress's hat. It was just like the roses Kai's family had grown, and everything came rushing back to her! She didn't say anything to the Sorceress, but once Gerda was alone again, she began to cry. She couldn't believe she had forgotten Kai when he needed her help.

Her tears fell onto the warm earth. A moment later, one of the rose bushes the Sorceress had hidden pushed up through the earth.

"Dear Gerda, why are you crying?" the rose bush asked, with a small voice like rustling petals.

"Because I have not found my friend Kai, and now I fear he might be dead," Gerda sobbed.

"Do not despair," the rose bush said. "I have been under the earth all of this time and I could see all of the dead. Kai was not there. Wherever he is, he isn't dead."

"Oh dear rose bush, I could hug you!" Gerda cried.

"Better not, my thorns will prick you," the rose bush chuckled. "But be careful of our mistress, the Sorceress. She hid me so you would forget Kai and she enchanted you to make you forget your home. Now go, find your friend!"

Gerda ran for it, straight out of the garden. She jumped over the fence and ran and ran until she could go no farther. She dropped to the ground in a small woodland and looked around her for the first time. She noticed, with a jolt, that it was nearly winter again—she had been in the Sorceress's garden for a whole year!

Two white doves swooped down and dropped a warm, red cloak in front of her. "We have news for you, Gerda," cooed the doves. "We know you are looking for Kai and we saw him the night he disappeared."

Gerda gasped in excitement. "You did?"

The doves told her that they had seen the Snow Queen kiss Kai so he would forget Gerda and his home, and how she had taken him away to Lapland.

"Lapland," Gerda whispered to herself. She had heard tales of the northern land, but she knew it was very far away. "I'll never get there," she said, sadly.

At that moment, a reindeer came trotting through the trees.

"Bae is from Lapland," explained the doves. "He can take you there."

"Oh, thank you for helping me!" Gerda cried.

She climbed onto Bae's back and the reindeer set off at a gallop.

It was a long and hard journey through the cold and the thick snow, but eventually they reached the palace of the Snow Queen. As they approached the gates, the Snow Bees saw them and attacked in a swarm. It was the strongest, coldest snowstorm that Gerda had ever known.

She and Bae battled through and emerged next to a lake of gleaming ice. In the middle of the lake sat the Snow Queen, on a jagged frozen throne. In front of her, crouched on the ice, looking blue with cold—was Kai!

"For the last time, Kai," the Snow Queen said. "If you can solve that puzzle and find the word I am thinking of, I will let you go home. Otherwise you must stay with me forever."

Kai was staring at shards of ice with letters scratched onto them. He kept pushing them around to rearrange them but he looked totally stumped.

Gerda ran up to him. "Kai! It's me, Gerda! I've come to take you home!" She kissed him on the face and hugged him.

Gerda's warm kiss melted the magic of the Snow Queen's kisses and Kai blinked at her. "Gerda? GERDA!" He stood up and hugged his best friend as hard as he could. Gerda took his hands and they spun around in circles, so happy to see one another. As they whirled around, they whipped up the ice shards Kai had been trying to rearrange.

"How DARE you come to my palace!" the Snow Queen thundered. "He will not be coming with you, for he cannot solve the puzzle."

Gerda looked down to see that the ice splinters had rearranged themselves into a word. "Oh really?" she retorted. "Is the word you were thinking of 'ETERNITY'?"

The Snow Queen roared with fury, for that was the word. Her spell over Kai was broken and the two friends and Bae raced out of the palace.

It was a long journey home. When they arrived back in the town, it was summer and their families had thought they were lost forever. Kai and Gerda were both older than when they had left, but their friendship was stronger than ever.

"Gerda never gave up on me," Kai told everyone.

Gerda smiled back at him. "And I never will."

Hua Mulan,
the Noble Warrior

Adapted from *Ballad of Mulan*, by Guo Maoqian

Once, long ago in China, there lived a young girl called Hua Mulan. She lived with her parents and her baby brother. Mulan always did her best to be a good daughter and loved her family dearly.

Mulan lived in a small kingdom, ruled by a kind king. This kingdom, and several others, were all ruled over by the Emperor of China. One day, a letter was sent to every household to say that each family would have to send a man to war. If they had a son the right age, he would be selected. Otherwise, the father would be taken.

Mulan's father read the letter aloud with a shaking hand.

As Mulan listened, worries started to swirl in her mind, for her father had not been well recently. She knew he would barely be able to lift a sword, let alone fight.

Mulan knelt in front of him and clasped his hands in hers. "Father, you are not well. I will speak to the army and I'm sure they will release you from this."

"Thank you, dear. I hope you are right," said her father, closing his eyes in relief.

Mulan knew that the army wouldn't be kind as she had said to her father. She had

heard many tales of old or sick men being dragged away to war and she was determined to save her father from that fate.

Two days later, Mulan arose before dawn. She dressed like a boy, made her hair look like a boy's, and picked up her father's sword, a traditional weapon called a dao. Then she slipped down to the village to wait.

Before too long, an army rounded the corner, led by a king and several generals on horseback. But it was not Mulan's own king who rode at the head. It was Dou Jiane, the king of the next-door kingdom. He had already collected all of his men and was riding to meet the Emperor.

Riding at his side was his daughter, Xianniang. She was most unusual in China, as she was a warrior herself. She was as strong and fierce as any man. When she saw Mulan standing at the roadside, she pointed. "Look, father, another soldier."

Her father waved this away. "We have all of our men. Leave him here for his own king."

Xianniang was looking Mulan up and down very carefully.

Does she see through my disguise? Mulan worried.

Finally, Xianniang spoke. "This soldier looks sharp and healthy. I want to take him for our own army. We can let the Emperor know he is with us."

Dou Jiane shrugged and agreed, so Mulan ran to join the end of the marching line of troops.

They marched for the whole day. Mulan kept her head down and didn't speak to the men on either side of her. As the sun set, they halted to make camp.

Just as Mulan was worrying about where she would sleep and whether her secret would be discovered, Xianniang appeared at her shoulder. "Come with me, young soldier."

Inside Xianniang's personal tent, the warrior princess stared at Mulan once again. "Soldier, have you fought before?"

"No," Mulan admitted, truthfully.

"Have you ridden?" Xianniang asked, sharply.

"No."

"Why have you come to fight?"

Mulan tried to make her voice deep. "My father is sick."

Xianniang leaned in close, her eyes raking Mulan's face. "Do you have other siblings?"

"A baby brother."

"And do you like being a big sister?"

"I do," said Mulan. A moment later, her mouth flew to her hand in horror.

"HAH!" cried Xianniang, "I knew it! You are like me, a warrior woman! Don't worry, I will keep your secret."

"I am not a warrior woman," Mulan said. "I was being truthful when I said I have never fought."

Xianniang's eyes gleamed. "Well, then, I will train you myself. We have two weeks until we meet the enemy."

From that moment on, Xianniang and Mulan were like sisters. Xianniang trained

Mulan hard, every day. Mulan grew strong. She learned to fight with a dao and to ride at top speed. Soon, she was holding her own when sparring with the other soldiers. Then, she began to beat them.

The day came when it was their turn to fight the enemy. Mulan's heart was in her mouth as they arrived at the battlefield and she saw the northern invaders lined up on the next hilltop, as far as she could see.

The battle was long and hard. Mulan fought without pause, back to back with Xianniang, sometimes fighting ten men at once between them. The girls used their smaller size to their advantage, weaving and ducking around the burly men.

Finally, they pushed the enemy soldiers back and back until a halt was called when the sun went down. Mulan and Xianniang returned to their camp, pleased with their day's work.

Several days the same as the first followed. The battles were long and hard, but Dou Jiane's army was winning and Mulan and Xianniang became famous as its best warriors.

Then, one night as Mulan lay sleeping, she was awoken by loud shouts of anger. Her hand flew to her dao and she jumped up, ready to fight, Xianniang at her side.

"Is it the northern invaders?" Mulan cried, squinting through the darkness as the shouts came closer. A group of men came into view dragging Dou Jiane!

"This man was found having secret talks with the enemy!" bellowed one man. "He planned to betray our emperor!"

"Father, tell me it isn't true!" Xianniang implored.

The men dragged him to the tent of the emperor. The gold and red silk tent flaps rustled as the emperor himself stepped out.

"Dou Jiane," said the emperor, his voice loud and deep. "Is it true?"

Dou Jiane was quivering as he said. "It is, your excellency."

"Then you will die at dawn for this great crime," said the emperor, sadly. "Such a shame. The king of our best army, with our two greatest warriors. Why would you betray what they have fought so hard for?"

Xianniang let out a sob of grief and raced away. Mulan rushed after her friend.

"How could he?" Xianniang wailed. "I cannot let him die, even if he did betray our Emperor."

"Do not worry," Mulan reassured her friend. "I have a plan."

The next morning, all the troops gathered for the execution.

Mulan and Xianniang stepped out of Xianniang's tent. They were both dressed in their girls' clothes and wearing their hair in the female way. They each held a knife in their teeth and walked silently.

Gasps followed them.

"That warrior is a woman?"

"Both our greatest fighters are girls?"

"How can it be?"

Mulan and Xianniang said nothing as they approached the Emperor in front of his tent.

Beside him, on the ground, knelt Dou Jiane. The executioner was ready and waiting.

"What is this?" the Emperor asked in confusion. "Who are you?" he demanded.

Mulan and Xianniang knelt before him. Mulan took her knife from her mouth and said, "Your Excellency, I am Mulan. I disguised myself as a boy to take my father's place in the war, for he is frail. I was selected and trained to be a great warrior by Xianniang. She is now my sister in arms. Although Dou Jiane betrayed you, he has also brought fame to your armies through his daughter, for Xianniang is one of your greatest warriors. Since Xianniang trained me, I am also a great warrior because of Dou Jiane. So, we ask for mercy for him. He is all Xianniang has."

The Emperor raised an eyebrow. "Dou Jiane would have thrown away all that you have fought for, and yet you still ask me to spare his life?"

Xianniang took the knife from her own mouth. "We do."

The Emperor stared at them both for a moment, then smiled. "And this is a spirit of true warriors. Mercy, especially for the weak." He raised his voice as he looked around

the gathered men. "We can learn much from these women. I will do what they ask and spare this man."

Mulan and Xianniang were thrilled! They thanked the emperor and Xianniang ran to her father.

The Emperor's mother, a famously wise lady, peered at Mulan closely. "It is not only mercy she shows, but protection. Mulan, you have shown that you will protect those in need, even at a great cost to yourself. You came to war to protect your father and you revealed your secret to protect Dou Jiane. I would like to reward you."

And so, when Mulan finally went home from the war, she rode the finest horse in the empire, laden with treasures that had once been beyond her wildest dreams. The legend of Mulan had spread even to her own village, but her family were still shocked when they saw her, because they had not dared to believe it.

Heidi's New Adventures

Adapted from *Heidi*, by Johanna Spyri

There once was a young girl named Heidi who lived in Switzerland many years ago. She was an orphan and she lived with her aunt, Dete, in a small town in the foothills of a mountain range called the Alps. Heidi missed her parents but she tried to tell herself that life with Dete was a new adventure, and they would have wanted her to make the most of it.

However, just as Heidi was starting to feel settled, Dete got a new job working as a maid in a smart house in the big city. She wasn't allowed to take Heidi with her, so she arranged for Heidi to go and live with her grandfather instead.

Heidi had never met her grandfather, but she had heard many tales of him and they made her nervous. He lived all by himself near the top of one of the big mountains. Because of this, not many people saw him, but those who did said he was very grumpy. Heidi was worried that she was going to be trapped alone on a mountaintop with a mean old man.

The morning of the dreaded day dawned bright and beautiful. They set

off from the closest village to Grandfather's house and then began to walk up, up, up until their legs burned. Heidi had never been so high in her life. The air was even more crisp and clear than lower down the mountains and the grass was bright green and lush. Grandfather's cottage looked rather pretty and Heidi found it hard to believe someone so bad-tempered could live somewhere so lovely—until the door flew open and she found herself staring into Grandfather's furious face.

He tried to send them away, but Dete firmly insisted that he take Heidi. As Dete left, she whispered. "Don't be afraid, he's a good man really."

Heidi took a deep breath. This was a new adventure.

To Heidi's surprise, Grandfather's cottage was rather homely inside and he had made up a bed for her, despite what he had said to Dete. Heidi said thank you and tried to chatter away as merrily as she could. Grandfather didn't answer much, but he didn't stop her talking.

When it was lunchtime, he was generous with food, and poured her a big glass of goat's milk. Heidi thought it was delicious and when she said so, the first hint of a smile cracked Grandfather's face. "That is fresh this morning from the goats outside. Their names are Little Swan and Little Bear. You can meet them after lunch, if you like."

"I should love to!" cried Heidi. She drained her glass and finished her lunch, then helped Grandfather to clear up.

"Good girl," he said, gruffly.

Outside on the mountain, Heidi had to get used to the feeling that she might fall off at every step. They were so high up and the slopes were so steep! But the two white goats were sure-footed as anything. Grandfather introduced her to a boy called Peter, who was the goatherd. "I'm pleased you're here," Peter beamed. "I have no friends my own age up here."

The two of them became firm friends very quickly. Grandfather didn't believe in school, so he taught Heidi what he knew at home and she spent her days out on the slopes with Peter and the goats, and her evenings with Grandfather, who wasn't mean at all. She grew strong on goat's milk and good food.

Then, one day, Dete wrote with the news that Heidi had been hired as a companion to a little girl called Clara, who had been very ill. She lived in Frankfurt. Heidi didn't want to leave the mountains for the big city, and Grandfather didn't want her to go either, but Dete wouldn't listen.

Arriving in Frankfurt days later, Heidi felt like a startled rabbit. The city air was warm and choked with fumes. Everything was so noisy. People chattered and shouted, engines rumbled, doors banged, dogs barked—and there were so many of all of them.

It's just another adventure, she told herself.

The big house was gloomy and ruled over by a mean housekeeper, called Mrs. Rottenmeier. She took Heidi to meet Clara. Clara was a few years older than Heidi. She was too weak to walk, so she had to lie in bed all day, every day.

Heidi felt lonely and scared. She may as well have been all alone in the big city for all any of the family cared about her. Nevertheless, she did her best to keep Clara company and soon the girls became friends. Heidi knew it must be hard for Clara to be cheerful when she was stuck in bed all day.

As time passed, Heidi tried her best to fit in with the household and be a ray of sunshine for Clara. But it was hard to do when she felt that her world was becoming increasingly dull and gloomy. She ached with homesickness for the mountains, for grandfather, and for Peter. She lost her appetite and grew thin. The healthy rosy blush faded from her cheeks.

One morning, Heidi went in to see Clara and found her looking frightened.

"Why, Clara, whatever is wrong?" Heidi asked.

"Last night, I saw a ghost!" Clara whispered. "It walked right past my door, all white and spooky!"

Heidi gasped, feeling very scared.

Mrs. Rottenmeier said there was no such thing as a ghost—until she saw the ghost the next night and woke the whole house up with her screams!

Heidi lived in fear of being visited by the ghost. She struggled to get to sleep and wished even more that she could escape to the mountains.

Then, one night, Clara woke to see the ghost again. This time, it didn't just pass her door but came right into the room. Clara screamed, but then stopped and gasped. "Why, Heidi, it's you!"

As lights flickered on all over the house and everyone came rushing to Clara's aid, they saw that the thin, pale, ghostly figure was in fact Heidi.

Heidi's eyes blinked open and she was very confused to find herself in Clara's room. "What's going on?"

"Heidi, you were sleepwalking. You were the ghost!" Clara told her.

The doctor was called right away. He took a long look at Heidi's pale face and tired eyes, and saw how thin she was. "I'm afraid this child is withering away in town," he told Mrs. Rottenmeier. "She must go back to the mountains right away before she becomes bedbound too."

Heidi was thrilled to go home. Almost as soon as she set foot on the mountain grass, the flush returned to her cheeks. After several days of good food and fresh air, she felt like herself again and was back racing around with Peter outside.

"What a miraculous recovery!" Grandfather laughed.

This gave Heidi an idea. "Grandfather, I think Clara should come to the mountains! Maybe it would make her better, too?"

Grandfather agreed that it was worth a try. Heidi wrote to Clara and all the necessary arrangements were made. A special wheelchair was brought so that Heidi could push Clara around on the mountain.

When Clara arrived, she was a little nervous at first.

"Just think of this as an adventure," Heidi said. Clara smiled.

As Heidi had hoped, Clara grew to love everything—the mountain village, the flowers, the goats, even Grandfather! Like Heidi before her, she grew stronger in the mountain air, eating good food.

Heidi and Clara were so inseparable that Peter began to feel jealous. He'd preferred it when it was just him and Heidi. He wished that they could go off and play by themselves.

One day, Heidi and Clara were sitting on the grassy slope by Grandfather's house, picking flowers and chattering. Clara's wheelchair sat a little way away. Peter crept up to it and pushed it down the slope before hiding behind a tree.

When Heidi saw the wheelchair racing down the hill, she jumped up to try to

catch it. But she was too slow. The chair hurtled toward some rocks and hit them at such high speed that it broke into pieces.

"My chair!" Clara wailed.

Heidi was crushed for her friend. Without a chair, Clara had no way to move around.

Peter felt ashamed of what he had done and ran home, crying.

Grandfather carried Clara back to the cottage and set her down in an armchair. He told the girls that it might be time for Clara to go home now.

"No!" said Clara. "I won't leave. I am so much stronger now. Look!" She pushed herself to her feet and stood, unsupported—if a little wobbly. Then, she took one step, then another.

"Clara that's amazing!" Heidi cheered.

The next morning, Peter came to the cottage with all of the parts of the wheelchair in a cart. He sheepishly admitted what he had done and said sorry to Clara.

"But Peter, you helped me," Clara said. "For now, I can walk!"

Peter, Clara, and Heidi spent a long time learning how to repair the wheelchair, and helping Clara to get strong enough to walk again.

When Clara's grandmother came up to visit, she was astounded to be met by the sight of her little granddaughter looking happy and healthy, walking down to greet her.

Heidi, Clara, and Peter all stayed friends for the rest of their lives and wherever they went and whatever they did, they looked upon everything as a new adventure.

Alice's Adventures in Wonderland

Adapted from *Alice's Adventures in Wonderland*, by Lewis Carroll

There once was a young girl called Alice, who lived in the English countryside. One late summer's day, she went for a walk with her older sister. They walked a long way and then sat down on the riverbank to each read their own books. Alice had a book of facts that she was very interested in, but as she read, she was distracted by a scurrying noise. She looked up and saw, with surprise, a white rabbit dressed in a smart jacket, hurrying past her.

Now, it was very strange to see a white rabbit that wasn't a pet. And even more strange to see it wearing clothes! Then, Alice's jaw dropped wide open as she heard the rabbit speak!

"Oh dear, I am very late," White Rabbit fretted. It pulled a tiny pocket watch out of its jacket pocket, checked the time, and shook its head before dashing on.

"Hello!" Alice called to White Rabbit, but it paid her no attention and ran on into the trees. Alice wondered what event a rabbit could possibly be late for! Her book forgotten, she scrambled to her feet and hurried after it.

She caught sight of it again just as it disappeared into a rather large rabbit hole between two trees. She knelt down and stuck her head into the rabbit hole. It was pitch black and she could see nothing at all. The hole really was enormous, big enough for her to crawl inside. She shuffled in a bit farther, then a bit more. "Hello, Mr. Rabbit?" she called.

There was no reply.

Alice pushed a little farther in, squinting in the darkness. And then suddenly, there was nothing under her hands and she fell forward, tumbling into black nothingness.

She landed, finally, with a big bump. "Oof!"

She was in a strange hall, lined with many doors of all shapes and sizes. Some looked big enough to let a giant through and others would barely fit Alice's own shoe. The White Rabbit was nowhere to be seen.

Alice looked for a door that seemed about her size and tried to open it. The handle wouldn't turn; it was locked. She tried every door in the hall, but they were all locked. She spotted a key on the floor and tried it in each door. Finally, it opened one, but the door was so small, Alice couldn't fit through it, even if she made herself into a tiny ball and breathed in.

Then, she noticed a small glass bottle filled with pink liquid sitting on a table. There was a label on the bottle, saying "Drink me."

Alice shrugged. She tipped the bottle back and drank it in one gulp. Instantly, she started to shrink smaller and smaller until she was the perfect size for the door!

Alice ran through the door and found herself outside. She wandered down a grassy lane until she happened upon a very strange sight. A small man wearing a huge top hat was sitting at a heavily laden tea table. Next to him was a hare and between them, curled up in a pretty porcelain teacup, was a sleepy-looking dormouse. There were many spare seats at the table. Alice went and sat in one.

"No room, no room!" The Mad Hatter and the Mad March Hare cried, shooing at her.

"There's lots and lots of room," said Alice, frowning.

"Oh well, if you're here, you might as well answer a riddle," said the Mad Hatter.

Alice was pleased. She liked riddles. "Go on then."

"Why is a raven like a writing desk?" the Mad Hatter asked.

Alice thought hard but she couldn't think of a clever answer. "I don't know," she said.

"Neither do we," giggled the March Hare.

Alice thought they were making fun of her and felt cross. "What's the point in wasting time asking riddles you don't even know the answer to?"

"TIME!" The Mad Hatter exploded. "Don't talk to me about him. We argued a few months ago and that's why it's always six o'clock."

"And that's why we're stuck at this never-ending tea party," said the Mad March Hare.

"I quite agree," said the dormouse, sleepily.

Alice stood up. "This is the stupidest party I've ever been to. I'm leaving."

She walked on and found herself in a garden, lined with white rose bushes. To her surprise, standing on one side of the garden, painting the white roses with red paint, were several live playing cards, just as tall as her.

"Hurry," one of the cards was moaning. "The Queen of Hearts will be here in a minute and she hates white roses."

Another card nodded as he hurriedly slopped paint on. "Only red will do!"

Before Alice had a chance to ask them what on earth was going on, a fanfare sounded and the most peculiar procession wound its way into the garden.

There were several more playing cards, lots of animals—including the white rabbit—and finally, a king and a queen, all dressed in red clothes covered with hearts.

That must be the King and Queen of Hearts, Alice thought to herself.

The Queen suddenly stopped, glaring at the freshly painted roses, which were dripping onto the ground below. "Who did this?" she demanded.

The playing cards who had been painting shuffled their feet. "Uh, we did, your majesty."

"OFF WITH THEIR HEADS!" the Queen bellowed. Then, she caught sight of Alice. "Who are you?"

"I'm Alice," said Alice.

"Play croquet with me," the Queen said.

"I'm not very good," Alice started.

"OFF WITH HER HEAD!" the Queen snapped.

"I mean okay, I'll try," Alice said, quickly.

She followed the queen out onto a croquet green, but

to her dismay, instead of being smooth and flat, it was all bumpy. She was handed a flamingo to use as a mallet and a hedgehog to use as a ball!

The game was impossible to play. The flamingos wouldn't stop curling their necks, the hedgehogs kept running away, and nobody was taking turns! Alice gave up and started chatting to the Cheshire Cat, an odd creature who looked just like a tabby cat but who could disappear at will, starting at his tail and ending with his wide, smiling mouth.

A playing card came running onto the green. "It's time for the trial!"

"What trial?" Alice asked, as everyone abandoned the game and rushed out of the garden. Shrugging, Alice followed them to a courthouse. The King of Hearts was the judge. As he walked in, the White Rabbit played a fanfare on a trumpet.

"Welcome to the trial of the Knave of Hearts," said the King.

The Knave cowered before the court.

As the trial began, Alice had the unpleasant feeling that she was growing again.

"Hey, stop growing. You're taking up all of the air," grumbled the sleepy dormouse next to her.

"Everyone grows," Alice scoffed. "I can't help it!"

"You, tall girl, come to the witness box," called the King of Hearts.

Alice didn't know why they were calling her since she'd never even seen the Knave before, but she got up anyway. On her way, she accidentally knocked over the witness box, sending the creatures inside sprawling. "Oops, sorry!" she said.

"Right, that's it," the King banged his gavel. "You must leave the court for this crime."

"What crime?" Alice demanded.

"Being too tall," replied the King.

Alice was fed up of being bossed around in this strange world. "That's a stupid rule," she said. "I'm not going anywhere."

"How dare you answer back to me?" the King cried. "Hold your tongue!"

"I will not," said Alice. "This whole place is silly and this trial is silly too. I bet the Knave was never near those tarts."

The Queen of Hearts drew herself up. "I'm sure YOU took them!" she shouted. "The Knave is pardoned. Off with her head!"

The card guards marched toward her, looking cross. Even though Alice was surrounded, she didn't feel scared. "Pooh, you're just a pack of cards," she said. "You can't do anything to me!"

The cards launched at her face, swarming all over her. Alice brushed them away, laughing—

And then opened her eyes to find herself lying on the riverbank. Her sister was brushing fallen leaves off her face.

Alice sat up. "I was dreaming?"

"Yes, for quite a while," her sister laughed. "I think you quite wasted the afternoon."

Alice thought about her adventures in the strange world and how she had learned to stand up for herself, even when she was surrounded by people telling her what to do. "*I* don't think so," she said, smiling to herself.

The Tale of
Athena's
Great Contest

Traditional story from ancient Greece

Once, a long, long time ago, there was a girl named Athena who was very clever and wise. She was also strong; she'd been born holding a spear, and few people could beat her in a fight. Athena was famous all over the ancient world for this, because she wasn't just any normal girl. She was the Greek goddess of wisdom and war. Her father was Zeus, the king of the gods and god of the sky. She lived with him and the other gods on top of a huge mountain, called Mount Olympus. Their palace was so high, it was in the clouds.

Although Athena was admired and revered by the humans in the lands below, to the other gods, she was simply one of the young girls in the family. Like all families, they had their quarrels. Athena argued a lot with her uncle, Poseidon. He was the god of the sea and was known for being competitive and moody.

Now, in those days, the country of Greece was not one nation, but many small island kingdoms. These kingdoms were beautiful but dangerous places to live. Monsters still roamed the earth, always searching for humans to capture or trick. If the humans were lucky, the gods would protect them from these monsters.

One day, the gods were all sitting together in their palace. They were in a room of pure white, with marble columns around the edge, open to the bright blue sky. Clouds swirled farther down the slope, hiding the palace from the view of the mortals living far below. Zeus sat at the head of the table, his broad shoulders crackling with blue electricity. Farther down the room, Athena sat primly, in a long white gown, wishing she'd chosen a seat farther away from Uncle Poseidon, who smelled of fish.

Hermes, the messenger god, reported that a new city was growing by the coast of the mainland. It was on a very high hill, called the Acropolis. The word was that the king there, Cecrops, wanted it to be the most beautiful city in the world.

Zeus waved a hand to part the clouds below the palace and the gods all peered down. Athena could see that the city was indeed beautiful. There were glistening white stone temples, towers, and pathways, all overlooking the shimmering blue sea. Athena loved beautiful things, so when Zeus announced that the new city should have a protector, she immediately stood up and volunteered.

To her annoyance, so did Poseidon.

"This new city will need good guidance as it grows," declared Athena. "They should look to me for that."

"Nonsense," growled Poseidon, shaking his trident. "What guidance can you give them that any of us couldn't? I am older than you, I have seen more of this mortal world, and besides, the city is by the ocean. It is mine by rights."

Athena laughed in her uncle's face. "You cannot claim something

because it's next to the sea. The whole world is beneath the sky, would you like Zeus to claim it all because of that?"

Zeus looked thoughtful at this and Athena quickly held up her hand, laughing. "Do not try, Father."

Zeus smiled at his daughter, indulgently. He enjoyed seeing his brother annoyed by her cleverness.

Poseidon's face was awash with fury as he jumped to his feet. "That city is mine and I will fight you for it, if I must!"

Athena faced him calmly. "I'm sure that won't be necessary. Let us ask the people whose protection they would prefer."

Poseidon glared at her one moment longer. Then, with confidence, he said, "Fine." He disappeared in a swirl of seawater.

With a roll of her eyes, Athena left the council and used her own godly powers to transport herself to the city. She appeared in front of the gates, next to Poseidon, who had already called King Cecrops out to talk.

Poor King Cecrops was quite scared by the two arguing gods when they asked him to choose between them. He knew that whichever one he didn't choose would be angry, and no mortal ever wanted to anger a powerful god! "Dear God and Goddess, I am so flattered that you value our opinion so," he said, politely, bowing before them. "But we cannot possibly choose which of you we prefer. Perhaps you, in your great power and wisdom, can decide who should be our patron and protector?"

Poseidon glared at Athena. "Very well, a battle it is then."

Athena calmly straightened her helmet and picked up her spear. "You are certain you wish to battle the Goddess of War for this prize?"

Poseidon hefted his trident. "Absolutely."

Athena saw Cecrops scuttle back to the safety of his city walls. She saw the faces of the people peering out, looking scared. She saw the care and hard work that had gone into every brick and she knew that it would not be right to risk damaging the city. Battles between gods were always destructive and long. She certainly wasn't afraid to fight her uncle, but she wondered if there might be a better way …

"Wait," she commanded her uncle, in a loud and clear voice. "I have a different idea."

"Hah!" Poseidon barked. "Scared after all!"

"Not at all," said Athena smoothly. "But perhaps the best way to choose who can take care of this city is to do something for its people. We each must present the citizens with a gift. Something useful for them. The people will decide whose gift is finest, and that is who will be their patron."

Poseidon chuckled. "Very well, a gifting contest it is. But you must know that as an elder, my powers far outstrip yours." He marched up to the top of the Acropolis, the highest point of the city, where the white buildings gleamed in the full glare of the sun. Raising his trident high, he smashed the end down onto the ground, causing it to crack. A fountain of water burst forth from the ground and arced high into the air.

All the people cheered and King Cecrops clapped his hands. The fountain was the most beautiful anyone had ever seen and water was a splendid gift! They needed it for the city to grow and thrive. Athena frowned to herself as the citizens flocked forward to play in the water. Perhaps she had underestimated her uncle?

A small girl cupped her hands to catch some and drink it. But a moment later, she spat it out! "Urgh, salty!" she cried.

The girl's mother tried some of her own. Her eyes widened. "It's seawater!"

The mood was flattened. The people knew they couldn't drink seawater or wash their clothes in it. Suddenly, the fountain didn't have many uses at all. King Cecrops still

bowed politely to Poseidon, not wishing to anger the sea god. Poseidon accepted his thanks, confidently.

It was Athena's turn. She thought deeply, willing her wisdom to help her. She knelt down upon the ground and started scratching in the earth.

"What are you doing, Niece?" chortled Poseidon. "Trying to dig a hole to hide in? Do not feel too ashamed of your failure. I shall taunt you about it for only a century or two."

Athena just smiled. She placed something in the shallow hole she had dug and covered it over. Then, she stood up and stepped back.

A moment later, a green shoot appeared. It grew incredibly quickly, thickening and browning until the people could see it was the trunk of a tree. Branches bloomed, leaves unfurled, and small green fruits could be seen hanging in the boughs.

"It's an olive tree!" King Cecrops exclaimed.

The people of the city crowded around the tree, cheering. They all knew an olive tree was the most useful plant to have. They could eat the olives or press them for oil and use the wood of the trees on their fires. The leaves would provide shade during the hot summer days.

It was clear to all that Athena was the winner. King Cecrops bowed at her feet to thank her for the gift and ask her to be the patron of the city, which would be named Athens after her. They would build a temple to worship her in, right there on the Acropolis.

Athena accepted graciously, although she wasn't able to resist shooting a smirk at her uncle.

Poseidon was quivering with fury. He hated to lose, but even he could see that Athena's gift had been the better one by far.

King Cecrops was anxious not to anger the god of the sea since his watery realm lapped at the foot of the city. He knelt before Poseidon. "My lord. We will build you a temple also and worship your name every day."

Poseidon nodded curtly. "See that you do." He glared once more at Athena. "If it had been a fight, I would have won," he snapped. Then, he disappeared in a swirl of seawater.

Athena shook her head, smiling to herself. She knew she could beat Poseidon in both brains and brawn, and she was sure she would have to prove that again very soon.

And so it was that Athena became the patron goddess of Athens and watched over it through many trials as it became the legendary city that we know today.

Dorothy's
Adventure in Oz

Adapted from *The Wonderful Wizard of Oz,* by L. Frank Baum

There once was a young girl called Dorothy who lived with her Uncle Henry and Auntie Em and her dog, Toto, on a farm on the wide, flat Kansas prairie. There was nothing but farmland for miles and miles. Dorothy often found life a bit dull.

One day, a cyclone came roaring across the prairie. Dorothy and her family dashed to hide in the safety of the storm cellar.

Just as she was about to scramble down the cellar steps, Dorothy heard Toto barking inside the house! "I can't leave Toto!" she cried and raced back to get him. Toto was cowering under a bed and as Dorothy tried to coax him out, the cyclone hit, whisking the house up into the air! Dorothy was very scared.

Eventually, it landed with a big bump and bright sunlight streamed through the windows. Dorothy ran to the door and opened it to see a beautiful land outside! There was green grass, tall trees filled with singing birds, bright flowers, and a babbling brook. She knew right away that she wasn't in Kansas anymore. She spotted three very small men and a tiny lady approaching the house. They smiled and waved at her.

They introduced themselves as the Good Witch of the North and the Munchkins. The Good Witch explained that they had come to thank Dorothy for killing the Wicked Witch of the East and setting their people free.

Dorothy was confused and told them she hadn't killed anyone, but they showed her that her house had crushed the Wicked Witch. Her feet were sticking out from beneath it, wearing silver shoes.

Unnerved, Dorothy asked them where she was and how she could get home to Kansas. The Good Witch told her the only way was to follow the Yellow Brick Road all the way to the Emerald City and ask the Wizard of Oz for help. Then, she touched Dorothy on the forehead to protect her from evil magic, and gave her the silver shoes to wear, explaining that the shoes were magic but nobody knew what they did.

Dorothy thanked them, then put on the silver shoes and set off down the Yellow Brick Road with Toto trotting next to her.

On the way, Dorothy met three strange creatures—a scarecrow with no brains, a tin man with no heart, and a cowardly lion. All three of them wondered if the Wizard of Oz could help them with their problems, the way that Dorothy hoped he might help her with hers. They joined her to walk to the Emerald City together.

Eventually, they arrived at the gleaming green Emerald City and asked to see the Wizard. He appeared as a giant, stern floating head. After he listened to their requests, he spoke in a loud, booming voice. "I will only grant what you have asked if you first defeat the Wicked Witch of the West. Do that and then return."

The friends left the city.

"But nobody has ever managed to defeat the Witch of the West," whimpered Lion.

"We can do it," said Dorothy. "After all, I defeated one witch in Oz without even trying. How hard can another one be?"

As the friends set off toward the Witch's castle, they had no idea that the Witch had already spotted them. She had only one eye, but it was as powerful as a telescope.

"Who are these intruders?" she muttered.

She sent her flying monkey servants to kill them. The monkeys swooped down

and picked up all of the friends. They pulled the stuffing out of Scarecrow and dropped Tin Man on the rocks so that he was all dented.

They took Lion and Dorothy back to the Witch's castle. The Wicked Witch saw the Good Witch's mark on Dorothy's forehead and knew she couldn't hurt her, so she decided to keep her prisoner instead.

The Witch locked Lion up in a cage and made Dorothy clean her castle. She noticed Dorothy's silver shoes and wanted them for herself. She waited for a moment to steal them, but Dorothy thought they were very pretty, and she never took them off. So, the Witch came up with a plan.

She laid an iron bar across the kitchen floor and used a spell to make it invisible. When Dorothy came walking through, she tripped and one of the shoes flew off her foot. The Witch caught it with a cackle.

Dorothy was annoyed by the Witch's trick. She picked up a bucket of water and threw it on the Witch, crying, "How dare you try to steal my lovely shoe?"

The Witch squealed as the water hit her and she began to melt away.

"How did you know my secret weakness?" she wailed as she melted into nothingness.

"I—didn't!" Dorothy gasped. But a moment later, she skipped with glee. "We did it!"

She and Lion ran out of the Witch's castle. They collected Scarecrow and put all his stuffing back in, then they picked up Tin Man and hammered out all of his dents.

They ran back to the Emerald City and crashed into the Wizard's reception hall. "We did it! We defeated the Wicked Witch! Will you help us now?"

"No," said the Wizard.

Dorothy stamped her foot and a screen toppled over to reveal a little old man speaking into a microphone. "I can't grant your—oh."

The man stopped as he saw them all staring at him.

"You're the Wizard of Oz?" Dorothy asked.

The man's face fell. "Well, yes, and no. I'm just a simple showman from Ohio. I used to take my hot air balloon around all the country fairs but one day I got blown far away and I landed here. The Ozians thought I was a wizard and I never corrected them. But really, I have no magical powers. Please don't tell anyone my secret!"

"But, our wishes ..." said Dorothy, sadly.

Now, the Wizard knew that the Scarecrow did have brains—the poor creature just didn't know it yet. And Tin Man had heart and Lion had courage, they just didn't feel it. If he could find a way to make them realize that, then their wishes would be granted.

He made a little cut in the top of Scarecrow's head and poured in lots of pins and needles before sewing it back up, saying "This will make you sharper." Then, he opened Tin Man's hinged chest and placed a silk heart stuffed with sawdust inside. Finally, the Wizard gave Lion a small bottle of liquid courage to drink.

Dorothy's friends all beamed. Scarecrow felt clever, Tin Man felt full of love, and Lion felt brave enough for anything. They thanked the Wizard for his gifts.

The Wizard looked turned to Dorothy. "You know, I think it's high time I went back home too. Ohio and Kansas aren't so very far apart. We can fly there together in my hot air balloon!"

The Wizard pulled out his old hot air balloon, made some repairs, and fired it up. Just as Dorothy was about to climb into the basket, Toto wriggled out of her arms to chase a kitten.

Dorothy couldn't bear to leave Toto behind in Oz, so she chased after him.

"Dorothy, the balloon won't wait!" the Wizard called, as it started to lift up into the air.

Dorothy caught Toto and ran back to the balloon, but it was too late. The balloon was high up in the sky and being whisked away by the wind.

"Oh no," cried Dorothy, with tears in her eyes. "Now I'm stuck here forever!" Although she loved her new friends dearly, she missed her Uncle Henry and Auntie Em.

Just then, the Good Witch of the North arrived and asked Dorothy why she was crying. When Dorothy told her, the Good Witch smiled. "I have been searching for answers for you and I discovered that those silver shoes can take you home. All you have to do is click your heels three times and say where you wish to go. You will be whisked straight there."

"Oh, thank you!" Dorothy cried. She hugged all of her friends and promised she would never forget them.

She picked up Toto and took a deep breath, then clicked her heels and said, "Auntie Em and Uncle Henry's house, Kansas."

Dorothy was whirled through the air, as if she was back in the middle of the cyclone. She landed with a bump and looked around her. She was back on the prairie! The storm was over and there was her house, the same as it had ever been.

"Toto, we're home!" She hugged the little dog tight.

Aunt Em stepped out of the house and Dorothy ran to hug her. She knew she would miss her friends and the exciting adventures of Oz, but there was no place like home!

hinemoa's
Great Swim

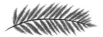

A traditional Māori story, from New Zealand

A long time ago, in ancient Aotearoa, there lived a girl called Hinemoa. She was the daughter of a Māori chief, Umukaria, and she was beloved by her whole tribe. They lived on the shore of the great Lake Rotorua. It was a wild and adventurous land, but Hinemoa did not tend to explore much. She knew her path in life and was happy to walk it. One day, she would be expected to marry the son of a chief from another tribe and go to live with them. Until then, she enjoyed sitting by the lake with her family.

Lake Rotorua was so large that in the middle of it was an island, called Mokoia Island, where another tribe lived. One day, the Mokoia tribe came to the shore for a great gathering. They all met in the meeting hall of Hinemoa's tribe, which was called a *marae*. The two tribes shared food, swapped stories, and danced. As Hinemoa danced, her eye was caught by a young man, standing on the edge of the marae. He was so handsome that she wondered how she had not noticed him at previous gatherings. When Hinemoa smiled at him, he smiled back and it was like his whole face was being lit by the sun.

Hinemoa found her feet carrying her toward him.

"Hello, Hinemoa," he said.

Hinemoa frowned. "You know me?"

The boy smiled. "Of course. You are the daughter of the chief, princess of your tribe. We all know who you are, beautiful Hinemoa."

Hinemoa blushed, partly because he had called her beautiful, but also because she didn't know who he was. "I am sorry—I cannot remember your name," she admitted.

"You cannot remember what you do not know," said the boy. "I am Tutanekai."

As their eyes locked, Hinemoa felt like she was flying. *So, this is love at first sight,* was all she could think as she gazed at him.

"Tutanekai," she repeated. "I am so glad to know you now."

They spent the whole meeting talking and laughing. It was as if they had been friends for their entire lives. When the tribes parted, Hinemoa was sad to say goodbye but she watched the canoes sailing back to Mokoia Island with a warm glow in her heart. She knew she had found the person she was meant to be with. She told nobody yet, for she knew that Tutanekai was not the son of the chief. She didn't want to hear anybody reminding her that she would not be allowed to marry a commoner.

The next time the tribes met, Hinemoa was so excited that she couldn't sleep the night before. She was up and waiting by the shore of the lake before the canoes had even set off. And when she saw Tutanekai climbing ashore, her heart skipped a beat. This time, he had brought his wooden flute to play at the gathering. Hinemoa couldn't ever remember hearing such sweet music.

Later on, they slipped outside the marae together. Hinemoa told Tutanekai that she loved him and he said that he loved her too.

"If only I were the son of a chief, we could be married," sighed Tutanekai.

"We can be married anyway," Hinemoa insisted.

Tutanekai looked doubtful. "Surely your parents will not allow it?" he said. "Even my tribe won't be pleased if I get above my station."

"We will talk to them," Hinemoa said, tossing her head. "We can persuade them."

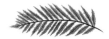

And so, the two young lovers went to ask the chiefs that same day.

When Hinemoa had finished speaking, Umukaria looked at his daughter sadly. "I am so sorry, Hinemoa, but it is not possible. Tutanekai is a fine man, but he isn't going to be a chief."

Hinemoa's eyes flashed. "I do not care! I could never love a chief the way I do Tutanekai."

Her father sighed. "It still is not possible."

"I agree," added Tutanekai's chief. "Such a marriage is impossible."

"I do not want this marriage for status," said Tutanekai. "I love Hinemoa for her, not because she is the daughter of a chief."

His chief looked at them both, with a sad smile. "Then you two have a true love. But we cannot change the rules. Now, it is time for you to come home."

Tutanekai was bundled into a canoe, while Hinemoa cried on the shore.

Umukaria ordered all of the tribe's canoes to be pulled far out of the water, so that Hinemoa couldn't take one and go after Tutanekai.

That night, as the moon and the stars shone down over the great lake, Hinemoa stared over at the shadowy shape of Mokoia Island. She knew that she could not obey her family and wait to marry a chief's son. She longed for Tutanekai and her heart was breaking under the weight of knowing she might never be allowed to see him again.

Just then, she heard a soft sound of a flute floating over the still surface of the lake. It was Tutanekai playing the same tune he had played for her the day they had met! She closed her eyes; the music made it easy to imagine that he was right there with

her. She stayed there and the music carried on playing, until the darkness began to turn into the pale morning.

Every night after that, Hinemoa would sneak out to look over at Mokoia. And every night, the beautiful flute music would come drifting over the lake, a message from her true love.

One night, Hinemoa could bear it no longer. Her heart ached for Tutanekai.

"If I can't use a canoe, I will swim to him," she said to herself.

Now, Hinemoa had lived on the shores of Lake Rotorua for her whole life. She knew the lake was vast and that the swim would be hard.

All of the children of her tribe could swim, but Hinemoa had always preferred paddling and splashing at the shore to swimming seriously. She decided that she should get better and stronger, so for weeks she rose early and swam farther and farther every day, until she was the best swimmer in her tribe.

She was still worried about quite how far the journey was. She knew if she could get something to help her float, that would make the journey easier, as she would be able to rest a while when she got tired.

She found a pile of hollow gourds that her tribe used as drinking flasks on the ground outside her hut. She took several of the gourds and tied them to her dress with twine. When she got into the water, the hollow gourds floated, as she had hoped.

Hinemoa quietly paddled out away from the shore. With the silver moon high in the sky and Tutanekai's music guiding her, she knew exactly where she needed to go.

She swam harder than she ever had in her life. It took a very long time, and the moon rose and set again while she swam on. The currents of the lake were strong, and several times she tired. But the sound of Tutanekai's music always pulled her on.

Eventually, when she was entirely exhausted, she arrived on the shore of Mokoia Island. She flopped down, panting and shivering. She knew that Tutanekai was so close but she barely had any strength to crawl.

On the shore of Mokoia were several pools where hot water bubbled out from deep underground. Hinemoa crawled to one of them and slipped in, letting the warm water

soothe her tired body. There, she pondered how she would find Tutanekai without alerting the rest of his tribe, for they would be sure to send her home.

Just then, a servant arrived at the pools. Tutanekai had sent him for water, so that he could carry on playing his flute on the hilltop for Hinemoa. The servant was

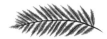

carrying a hollow gourd to fill, just like the ones Hinemoa had used for her great swim.

As the servant approached, he could see the shape of someone sitting in one of the pools. "Don't mind me," he said. "I am just here to fetch water for Tutanekai and then I will be gone."

As he dipped the gourd into the water, Hinemoa hit it with her fist and broke it.

"What are you doing?" the servant cried in anger. "You wait until I tell Tutanekai, whoever you are!" he hurried away.

Hinemoa smiled to herself. A few moments later, the flute music stopped. And a few more moments after that, she heard footsteps approaching the pools.

"Who are you and why did you attack my servant when he was bringing me water?" Tutanekai demanded.

Hinemoa climbed out of the pool to be reunited with her true love.

Tutanekai wrapped her in his arms and they went to find her some dry clothes.

When the morning sun rose and the tribe found that Hinemoa was there, Tutanekai told them of her great swim across the lake.

His chief looked thoughtful. "In that case, it seems to me that your love is stronger than rules. If it cannot be defeated by the lake itself, I don't see how our tribe can stand in its way."

He sailed Tutanekai and Hinemoa over to the shore himself. Her anxious family had been searching for her, but when they heard the tale, Hinemoa's parents agreed.

And so, thanks to Hinemoa's bravery and determination, she and Tutanekai were together for the rest of their happy lives.

Chimidyue and the Butterfly

A traditional Ticuna story, from South America

There once was a young girl named Chimidyue. She lived with her family in a clearing in the Amazon rain forest. The wide, strong Amazon river gushed right past their clearing on its long, winding journey to the sea.

Chimidyue's entire family—parents, grandparents, siblings, aunts, uncles, and cousins—all lived in one big house in the middle of the clearing, called a maloca. Every night, they gathered to eat, talk, and sleep. During the day, everyone went their separate ways. The older family members went into the forest to fish and hunt. Chimidyue and the other young children had to help with the household chores or weeding the vegetable patches. It was against the rules for the children to go into the forest.

"You can get lost in moments and never find your way back," Chimidyue's mother told her. "And besides, it's full of vicious animals and evil spirits."

Chimidyue listened to her mother's advice, but she often peered through the huge trees, hoping to see something as exciting as a vicious animal or evil spirit. One day, she was sitting outside the maloca, weaving a basket. A beautiful big blue morpho butterfly

hovered right in front of her. Sunlight flashed off its bright wings.

"You look magical," Chimidyue whispered, as the butterfly danced through the air. "I do wish I could be like you!"

The butterfly twirled in the air, as if it was pleased. Then, it fluttered toward the edge of the clearing.

Chimidyue followed it, giggling and flapping her arms. Her basket was forgotten on the ground.

The butterfly carried on flitting, going between two big trees, then under a vine, around a bush, and over a fallen tree trunk. Chimidyue followed, trying to copy the way it could fly and float.

Finally, the butterfly passed between some vines and disappeared. Chimidyue blinked. It was like she had been dreaming and was just waking up, but she had followed the butterfly deep into the forest—and she had no idea which was the way home!

"Mother! Father! Help!" she called into the trees. "It's Chimidyue, I'm lost! Help!"

But nobody came to her.

Chimidyue did her very best not to panic. "Perhaps I can find a path," she told herself.

She started to walk, and after a while, she heard a sharp tapping noise. "Maybe that is someone working in the forest?" she said to herself, hopefully. But it turned out to be just a woodpecker, tapping away at a tree trunk.

"If only you were human, I'm sure you could show me the way home," Chimidyue sighed.

The woodpecker glared at her. "I don't have to be human to do that," it snapped. "I know exactly where you live."

Chimidyue clasped her hands together. "Oh, could you please show me?"

"Of course not, I'm busy," said the woodpecker, turning back to the tree trunk. "You wretched humans think we're all just here to serve you. I am just as important as you. You've got yourself lost, so you can find your way back."

Chimidyue walked on, feeling uncomfortable. She had expected vicious beasts but she hadn't known that the animals of the forest thought that humans were so conceited and selfish.

As she walked on, she heard other animals muttering. Some moaned about how humans had cut down their tree homes, others about how humans had hunted and killed their relatives.

I never thought about it like that … Chimidyue thought to herself.

As she walked, she still had no clue which way home was, and she was starting to get hungry. A spider monkey troop was climbing through the trees above her, picking fruits. One of them dropped some juicy fruit and Chimidyue scooped it up to eat.

"If I follow these monkeys, at least I won't starve," Chimidyue told herself. "Monkeys always know where to find fruit."

So, she walked along beneath the monkeys, picking up any fruit that they dropped. The sun began to sink low in the sky and Chimidyue still had no idea how to find her way home. She could hear the night creatures of the forest waking up and felt scared.

"Still, monkeys know how to stay safe from jaguars," she murmured. "I'll watch where they go to sleep and I'll sleep there too."

So, as the light faded, Chimidyue carried on following the monkeys through the forest. When the sun had almost set completely, she saw the monkeys start to climb down from the trees. To her

surprise, as each monkey's paws touched the ground, it changed into a human!

"Why, Chimidyue, it's you!" said a monkey man in a friendly voice. "What are you doing here?"

Chimidyue struggled to find words. "I, I, I—followed a butterfly and then I got lost and now I can't find my way home."

A kindly monkey woman smiled at her. "Don't worry, we can take you home tomorrow. Tonight, you are welcome to come with us."

"We're going to a festival. We've been invited by the Lord of the Monkeys."

"Oh, thank you, thank you!" Chimidyue cried, relieved to have found help at last. She followed the monkey people through the forest and soon they arrived at a big maloca, lit by big wooden torches.

Inside the maloca sat the Monkey Lord, in his human form. He frowned when he saw Chimidyue. "Human, why have you come to my festival?"

"We invited her," said the monkey woman.

The Monkey Lord grunted and said no more, but he was nowhere near as friendly as the other monkey people.

More and more monkey people arrived. They were all walking in human form, but many of them had wooden monkey masks on, or had painted their faces with black paint. They all greeted each other cheerily and drank together.

The Monkey Lord arose. "Now it is time for the dancing," he announced.

Several monkey people began to beat drums and shake rattle sticks. Others sang or played flutes. And everyone else began to dance.

Chimidyue stood shyly at the side. She didn't feel confident enough to join in, but she was amazed. *Their festival is just like the ones we have at home*, she thought.

The dancing went on for hours and hours. Then, everyone began to tire and went to their hammocks for the night. The monkey lady fixed up a small hammock for Chimidyue next to hers.

Chimidyue climbed in, her mind whirring from her strange day in the forest. She tried to go to sleep, but the Monkey Lord was snoring loudly nearby and the noise kept her awake. As she lay in the darkness, listening to him, she heard the Monkey Lord muttering in his sleep!

Curious, Chimidyue pricked up her ears.

"I will eat Chimidyue. I will eat Chimidyue," the Monkey Lord murmured again and again in his sleep.

Chimidyue squinted through the darkness and saw that he was covered in black spots. He was changing from human form—into a sleeping jaguar! He wasn't a monkey at all!

Chimidyue slipped out of her hammock as quietly as she could and grabbed one of the torches. She ran away through the trees, trying to get as far away from the jaguar as possible.

When dawn began to push through the leaves, Chimidyue stopped at last to rest. She still had no idea where she was and she was very tired and scared.

"It seems that every animal in here wishes me harm," she said.

"Now you know how we feel about humans," said a tiny voice.

Chimidyue looked up to see the big morpho blue butterfly sitting on the branch above her. "You again!" she gasped. "You led me here!"

"You followed me for fun," said the butterfly. "And I think you have learned much about the forest, little one. It is much bigger than your human world. Every creature in here has their own life, wants, and needs. They will not always behave how you want them to."

Chimidyue nodded her head. "We share the forest; it is not ours to use just as we want," she said.

The butterfly flapped its wings. "Exactly. I think it's time to go home. Follow me."

It fluttered its wings faster than Chimidyue had ever seen before and began to glow an even brighter blue.

Chimidyue felt herself shrinking, shrinking. Then, she looked down. Her arms were gone and she had two beautiful blue wings. "I'm a butterfly too!" she exclaimed.

The morpho butterfly led her through the forest and over the wide river to her home clearing.

"This is so much fun!" said Chimidyue. "I wish I could be a butterfly forever!"

"You belong with your family, Chimidyue," said the butterfly. "But now that you have been one of us, I hope that you will keep the forest in your heart and be mindful of how you treat us animals."

Chimidyue touched the ground and instantly changed back into her human form.

"I will," she promised the butterfly.

From that day on, Chimidyue always made sure that she and her family respected the animals who shared their forest home.

The Fountain, the Oven, and the Goddess

A traditional folk tale, from Romania

In a small house in the Romanian countryside lived a girl, called Elena, and her father. Elena was very kind and hardworking. Her father was a mild man and relied a lot on Elena to make decisions and take care of him and the house.

After many years of living like this, Elena's father remarried. Elena was pleased at first. She welcomed her new stepmother, and her new stepsister, Anca, who was the same age as her. She hoped they could grow to be as close as sisters could be.

But Elena's stepmother had other ideas … She made Elena do all of the work around the house and found fault with everything she did. Meanwhile Anca barely lifted a finger, but her mother praised her all the time.

Elena made and cleaned up breakfast and lunch and dinner for everyone. In between, she cleaned the whole house, chopped the firewood, looked after the animals, and did the laundry. But nothing was good enough for her stepmother.

"My breakfast is cold," she complained one morning, when she finally came to the table after she'd spent ages braiding Anca's pretty hair.

"Call that clean?" she sniffed, as Elena scrubbed at the floors to try to clear up the mud that Anca had tracked in from her morning walk.

"Be more careful with my dresses," she snapped when she saw Elena doing the laundry. "They are most delicate. Don't treat them like your rotten old clothes."

Elena felt furious at these words. She had done her best to fit in with her stepfamily, for her father's sake, but now she turned to him. "Father, I am trying my best. Can Anca not do some of this work?"

"Anca does so much for this family," crooned Elena's stepmother. "She is a light in this gloomy world. Stop whining."

Elena's father just huddled on his chair, looking nervous of his wife.

At that moment, the fire went out. "I will not fetch the firewood by myself," Elena declared. "Anca, you must help."

"I got the last load," said Anca, lolling in her chair.

"No, you didn't!" Elena cried. "You haven't even been to the woods since you arrived!"

"Stop trying to take credit for Anca's hard work, Elena," her stepmother snapped.

"Well done, Anca," Elena's father murmured.

That was the final straw. Elena marched out, slamming the door behind her.

They do not care for me, she thought to herself. *I must find somewhere else to live.*

So off she went down the road. She had been walking for a while when she saw a fountain that had been neglected and was clogged with leaves.

"Young girl, if you help me now, I will reward you later," said the fountain, in a tinkly voice. Elena had never encountered a talking fountain before, but her instinct was always to be kind. She got down on her hands and knees and removed all the leaves and scrubbed the fountain until it shone. Beautiful, crystal clear water sprang from it and Elena knew she had done a good job.

She walked on until she found an old oven, which was filthy and full of holes.

"Please, will you fix me?" The oven asked. "I will reward you later."

Elena cleaned all of the old grease off the oven and fixed the holes in it. Then, she walked on and on until she came to a beautiful meadow, bursting with pretty wildflowers an insects and birds busying around. An old lady was walking through the meadow. She waved at Elena when she saw her. "Young girl, what are you looking for?"

"I have had to leave my home," Elena explained sadly. "My stepmother makes me work all day and then credits my stepsister, Anca. I am not afraid of hard work, but I hope to do it in a place where it is appreciated."

The old lady smiled. "I am the Goddess of Nature and if you help me today, I will make sure you are handsomely rewarded tomorrow. Will that do?"

Elena was surprised, but nodded. "Yes, what would you like me to help with?"

The goddess pointed through the trees to the edge of the meadow, where there stood a large stone house. "In my house over there, I have many children that need taking care of, but I must go out today to tend to my meadows and forests. I need you to wash and feed my children and have dinner ready for me when I come home. Can you do that?"

"I can," said Elena, eagerly.

"Lovely," said the goddess. "The children are out playing at the moment. Fill the bathtub in the courtyard and then call them to you. Thank you, Elena." She turned and carried on through the meadow.

Elena approached the rather grand stone house. She hurried through to the courtyard where she found a huge bathtub. She filled it, as the goddess had said, then raised her voice. "Children! It's bath time!"

There was a thundering noise and, to Elena's shock, dragons and wild beasts of every kind poured into the courtyard, all covered in mud from their games.

"These are the goddess's children?" Elena gasped.

She did her best to hold her nerve as the first dragon climbed into the bath and waited for a soaping. It took a while—and there was a lot of splashing—but soon Elena had bathed every wild beast there.

Next, she went inside and cooked the biggest pie she had ever made! The beasts ate it all up, growling with happiness. While they were eating, Elena made a second, smaller pie for the goddess.

When the goddess returned, she was very pleased indeed. "You have taken such good care of my children, Elena," she exclaimed. "Thank you! Now, go upstairs and pick out a chest. Take it home to your father's house. I promise this will make things better. There is just one rule: You mustn't open the chest until you get home."

Elena climbed up to the steep stairs to find dozens of wooden chests. Some of them looked very fine indeed and were covered with jewels. Elena didn't feel worthy of such fine things, so she chose the ugliest, oldest-looking chest. She thanked the goddess and went on her way.

On her way back, Elena was tired, hungry, and thirsty. She had been so busy making food for the beasts and the goddess that she hadn't had anything to eat or drink herself!

When she passed the little oven, it was full of delicious cakes for her to eat, as a thank you for helping it. Elena ate several cakes, gratefully, until her stomach stopped rumbling.

Next, she came to the fountain. On the edge of the fountain stood two silver goblets. The fountain invited her to drink as much as she would like. Elena drank until she was thirsty no more.

When she arrived back at the house, her father ran out to greet her. "Elena, I have missed you!" he cried. "I wish I had not let you go. I was wrong to dismiss all your hard work."

Elena hugged her father tightly. She explained to him where she had been and how she had come by the chest she was lugging. Together, they opened it and dozens of cows, sheep, pigs, and horses climbed out.

"My goodness, we are rich!" Elena's father cried. "Thank you, Elena, you clever, hardworking girl!"

Elena's stepmother glared at the animals. She was speechless, for she could not deny that Elena had done something very good indeed.

"Pooh, if Elena can find such things, I'll get even better ones," said Anca. "Just you wait."

"Yes, well done Anca," said the stepmother as Anca left the house. "You will beat Elena easily, as you always do."

As Anca walked, she passed the blocked-up fountain and ignored its pleas for help. She'd never really cleaned anything in her life and she wasn't about to start now!

She ignored the broken oven, too. Even if she had known how to fix it, she was too lazy to do it properly.

In the meadow, she met the goddess and was given the same task as Elena. Anca had never given anyone else a bath before. She made the water far too hot and all of the dragons and beasts were scalded when she tried to dip them in. They yelped with pain and ran away.

Anca shrugged. "Fine, stay dirty then."

Next, she started to cook dinner, but she burned everything and everybody lost their appetites.

When the goddess came home, she saw what Anca had done. As she had done with Elena, she invited Anca to choose a chest from the attic. Anca went straight to the biggest, most exquisite-looking chest and picked it up, then ran away before the goddess could change her mind.

When Anca arrived home, her mother greeted her joyously. "Here is my precious Anca, with the real riches!"

Anca opened the chest, and a full-grown, three-headed, very angry dragon streamed out of it. It chased Anca and her mother out of the house and far away. They were never seen again and Elena and her father lived happily ever after.

The Tale of Odette, the Swan Maiden

Adapted from *Swan Lake*, by Pyotr Ilyich Tchaikovsky

There once was a girl called Odette, who lived in a cottage on the edge of a vast, enchanted forest, which was ruled over by a wicked soceror called Rothbart. Odette loved to explore. Heedless of danger, she would often lead her friends on daring adventures to find the deepest, darkest secrets among those trees.

One day, Odette led her friends to a clearing by a strange, still lake, farther into the forest than they had ever gone before. The other girls felt scared and wanted to go back. But Odette was fascinated by the crystal waters of the lake. It was a very hot day, and they had walked far, and the gentle waves lapping at the shore were so inviting. She would not turn back and instead dipped her toe into the cool water.

An owl had been watching them from a tree branch near the shore. With a flurry of feathers, it launched from the tree branch and transformed into the figure of a man. Odette gasped—it was Rothbart, the famous evil sorcerer! With a wave of his hands, he turned Odette and all of her friends into swans.

"Hah, now you shall swim on my lake forever," he chuckled. "This is my lake, and

I curse anyone who uses it without my permission. You will be squabbling swans by day and miserable humans by night. No matter where you fly by day, at nightfall you will magically return here. The curse will only be broken if one who has never loved before vows to love Odette forever."

Odette was horrified to have brought this awful curse down on her friends. When she reverted to her human form that night, she explained her plan to them.

Every day, the flock of swans flew as far out of the forest as they could, and every day they tried and failed to lure someone back with them before night fell and they were magically pulled back to the enchanted lake to take their human forms.

Meanwhile, in a grand nearby palace, poor Prince Siegfried was being given some unwelcome news.

"You are a man now," pronounced the Queen. "It is long past time you found yourself a bride and settled down."

"But I just haven't met anyone I want to marry," Siegfried protested.

"It isn't about what you want," said the Queen, sternly. "You *must* marry. We will hold a royal ball tomorrow night and you shall pick your bride from the girls I invite."

Prince Siegfried felt angry at his mother's words. His friend Benno tried to cheer him up. He pointed at a flock of white swans circling overhead and suggested they went hunting in the forest. Siegfried and Benno grabbed their bows and set off in pursuit of the birds. The swans flew fast to the trees. Siegfried ran into the forest, chasing the swans for all he was worth, until eventually, the light faded. Benno gave up and went home, but Siegfried carried on.

Up in the sky, Odette could see that the sun was nearly setting. "Quick, quick," she urged her friends. "We must go to the lake now so that we can transform."

Just as dusk fell, Siegfried emerged in the quiet clearing. He saw the still lake and then raised his bow as the flock of swans touched down onto the water. To his surprise, one of them swam right up to him and then, with a shadowy shimmer, transformed into a beautiful maiden wearing a dress just as elegant as her swan feathers had been.

Siegfried dropped his bow in shock.

"Please don't shoot me or my friends!" said Odette.

"I won't," promised Siegfried. "But how are you both a swan and a human?"

Odette sighed and explained the curse to him. Siegfried felt delighted to be meeting such an interesting girl, but he was horrified to hear of her fate. "And is there any way of undoing this spell?" he asked.

"There is only one," Odette admitted. "One who has never loved before must swear to love me forever."

"And you have no power over that," Siegfried mused. He thought of the order his mother had given him. "I know a little of how that might feel."

At that moment, Rothbart swooped into the clearing as an owl, then transformed into his human self. "Who are you and what do you want with my swans?" he demanded.

Siegfried frowned. "Is this the sorcerer who has put this curse on you?" he asked Odette.

"He is," she confirmed, sorrowfully.

Siegfried raised his crossbow once more. "Then I shall kill him and release you."

Rothbart roared with anger and Odette cried, "No!" She moved between Siegfried and Rothbart. "If Rothbart dies before the curse is broken, it can never be undone!"

Rothbart laughed. "True. Not that it will ever be undone anyway, my dear Odette."

With that, the evil sorcerer left. Odette and her friends looked fearfully at Siegfried's bow, so he broke it in two over his knee. The swan maidens relaxed.

"Well, you must know what it is the girls hope for," Odette said, honestly. "They hope that you will be the one to save us. But I think it's just nice to have new company after all this time."

Siegfried was touched by her honesty and sweetness. He knew if he had been given a magical way to get out of his fate, he would have grabbed it with both hands.

The two of them linked arms and walked into the forest, chatting away as easily as if they were old friends. To anyone who was watching them, it would have been clear that that Siegfried and Odette were falling in love. But all too quickly, the bright fingers of dawn were reaching through the wood and Odette was whisked magically away from Siegfried and back to the lake, where she became a swan once more.

When Siegfried went home, he couldn't forget Odette. The whole of the next day, she was on his mind and he began to dread the ball that evening even more. Before, he had not wanted to get married at all. Now, he knew he only wanted to marry Odette.

But, despite his dread, all too soon he found himself dressed up in the royal ballroom, meeting all the girls his mother had rounded up. Siegfried barely looked at them, until he heard a voice say, "May I introduce Odette?"

He spun round to see the girl whom he had been thinking about all day smiling at him. "Odette!" he cried, taking her hands in his. "Mother, this is who I would like to marry. I promise I will love you forever, Odette."

Siegfried's mother was delighted and Odette's father, who stood with a protective hand on her shoulder, looked very pleased as well.

But what Siegfried didn't know is that he was not looking at Odette at all ...

Odette had been swimming up and down on the lake, waiting for the sun to set. She hadn't stopped thinking about Siegfried all day. The instant that the sun set, Odette set off at a run. The journey was far, and the forest was full of wolves and other wild beasts. She and the other maidens had never dared venture far from their lake in the darkness, but now Odette had no choice.

She jumped over fallen tree trunks, ducked under branches that grabbed at her hair, swerved away from a racing stag, and hid from a prowling bear. And then she ran and ran.

As the moon rose high, she arrived at the palace to find the doors were locked! Desperate, she ran around the side of the palace to the window. Inside, she saw Siegfried embracing another maiden who looked just like her! Next to Siegfried, she saw a man and, despite his magical disguise, she knew that it was Rothbart.

Odette hammered on the window, calling for Siegfried. She hit it again and again until the glass broke. She stumbled into the ballroom as everyone turned to stare. "Siegfried, it's me, Odette! That girl is a fake," Odette gasped. "I love you!"

Siegfried looked uncertain. "She is?"

"Was she not here before the sunset?" Odette asked.

Siegfried dropped the other Odette's hands, with a gasp. Instantly, her face transformed—to reveal that she was Odile, Rothbart's daughter! Rothbart dropped his magical disguise. "You stay away from my swan!"

Siegfried and Odette ran to one another. "I promise that I will love you forever and ever, Odette," said Siegfried.

"And you have never loved before," said Odette, with a smile. Together, they left the ball, climbed onto Siegfried's horse, and rode away into the dark forest.

As they rode, the sun rose and Odette was thrilled that she didn't transform back into a swan. They arrived at the lake to find the other swans waiting for their friend. They squawked and flapped with excitement when they saw that Odette was in her human form. As Odette and Siegfried kissed, all the other swan maidens transformed back into themselves.

Odette and Siegfried lived happily ever after. Odette had learned her lesson about venturing too far, but she and Siegfried never stopped having adventures.

Lykke,
the Little Mermaid

Adapted from *The Little Mermaid*, by Hans Christian Andersen

There once was a kingdom of merpeople, living deep in the sea. The king of the merpeople had six daughters. He tried his best to keep them away from the surface waters and the human world, but his youngest daughter, Lykke, was very curious about it. She wanted to see humans walking with their strange stick legs and their dry, fluffy hair. She wanted to see the giant ships they used to travel the oceans and the smaller boats they used for fun. She wanted to see what dry land looked like!

One day, she sneaked off to the surface by herself and spotted a big ship. She swam closer to take a look and saw a man on the ship, wearing a golden crown—the human prince. He was the most perfect thing Lykke had ever seen in her entire life.

She was so enchanted that she barely noticed when the waves started to become stronger and the wind whipped up. Before Lykke knew it, a storm had blown in and the ship was being tossed about on the waves, as if it were a scrap of seaweed. It was thrown onto some nearby rocks, smashing a hole in the bottom. The sea rushed in and Lykke gasped as she saw the prince, thrashing among the waves.

Lykke didn't even think about what she was doing. She shot through the sea, like a

dolphin through a school of fish. Her prince was sinking through the water, lifeless, his eyes closed. Lykke threw her arms around him.

She swam desperately toward the shore. She broke from beneath the waves, onto a sandy beach, and hauled the prince out of the water. With his eyes closed, he looked as if he was sleeping. She retreated back into the sea and watched, hoping a human would come and find him. Soon enough, three human women rushed down to the shore. They clapped the prince on the back and fussed over him until his eyes opened and he coughed up lots of water.

Lykke listened as the prince told the women about his voyage. He was an explorer. Lykke felt a rush of joy at having discovered this kindred spirit.

As she swam back home, she said to herself, *I must find a way to see him again.* She felt that she had seen her future and she was sure that it was exploring the human world with the prince by her side. She wondered what strange creatures lived on the land with the humans—she'd heard lots and lots of stories but she really wanted to see for herself.

Back in her home kingdom, Lykke wondered what to do. Finally, after many days of thinking and pining, she remembered that there was a Sea Witch who was said to have once walked on land, with humans.

The Sea Witch lived in a quiet cave at the very, very bottom of the ocean, right on the edge of the merpeople kingdom. Lykke didn't know how to get there, but she knew it was in the east, so she set off in the direction in which the sun rose each morning. She swam for days, and she was resting on a rock, exhausted, when she saw a pod of dolphins.

The dolphins were great friends of the merpeople, and liked to sing songs and tell tales of the places they had visited and the sailors they had met. Lykke enjoyed learning more about the humans she was so desperate to meet and the world she was so excited to see! They shared their food with Lykke, and tried to persuade her that being a mermaid was more fun than being a human, but, eventually, the dolphins showed her the way to the entrance of the Sea Witch's seabed cave.

The Sea Witch was curious to have a visit from one of the princesses, and astonished when Lykke told her what she wanted.

"I can indeed give you legs, if that's what you wish," said the Sea Witch, softly. "But Lykke, you must understand that all magic demands a sacrifice. In order to have legs, you must give up something else—your voice."

Lykke was taken aback. "Forever?"

"Perhaps," said the Sea Witch, seriously. "You tell me you do this for the love of a human. If this human kisses you, your can have your voice back. But there is something else. You cannot reverse this magic and have your tail again, unless the two of your marry. If you marry, you will have the choice to both live on the land or in the sea. But if you do not marry, you will be stranded on land forever."

"To live on land forever would be worth it, for him," Lykke smiled.

"Very well," said the Sea Witch. "Drink this potion and you will transform."

As soon as Lykke swallowed the glowing potion down, a great tingle went through her tail and her throat.

She was surrounded by a magical glow, and when it faded, her tail had been replaced by two human legs. She found that she could no longer breathe and kicked up to the air.

The Sea Witch surfaced beside her. The old mermaid pointed toward the shore. "Go quickly. Soon you will find it hard to swim."

Lykke tried to say thank you, but no words would come, so she smiled her thanks at the witch.

A short while later, Lykke arrived at the beach where she had left the prince days before. It felt strange to plant her brand-new feet upon the sand and stand up. She walked, with a few wobbles, up the beach. To her delight, she saw the prince himself walking toward her.

He cried out when he saw her. "Have you just come from the sea?"

Lykke nodded, with a smile.

"Having a swim?" the prince said. "I'm scared of it myself. I nearly drowned a few days ago. Strangely, I feel that I should thank you—although I don't believe we have ever met before!"

Lykke shook her head.

"I'm Prince Emil. What's your name?"

Lykke just smiled again and shrugged.

Prince Emil laughed. "Would you like to walk with me? It's nice to have company, even if it's quiet."

And so, they walked together. Lykke felt the warm sun on her skin. She saw grass, trees, and buildings. She heard birds singing, Emil introduced her to his dog, and she met the royal horses playing in the paddock. All the while, Emil chatted away to her. Lykke had never had a better afternoon and she didn't want it to end.

Neither, it seemed, did Emil. As the sun started to set, he invited her to dinner.

When dinner was over, he asked if she would like a room of her own in the palace. Lykke stayed that night and for every day after. Even though she could not speak, she and Emil grew close. Lykke sometimes missed her family, but she found she didn't miss life in the sea at all.

One day, Lykke found Emil looking nervous. "My parents say it is time to put my travels behind me," he told her, "and marry the princess of another kingdom."

Lykke felt her heart would sink right down into her beloved new feet. She shook her head at Emil, as tears began to roll down her face.

Emil wiped one away. "I hoped you might think that," he whispered. "For I told them that I could not marry her, when I have already found my soulmate."

He leaned in and kissed her. When they broke apart, it was as if someone had poured a cool drink down Lykke's throat, and she felt that she might try using her voice. She took a deep breath, and said "Emil, my name is Lykke."

Emil gasped with joy. "You can speak!" he cried.

Lykke nodded out of habit, then laughed. "Yes, I can!"

She told him the whole story of how she had come to be there.

By the end, Emil was gawping at her. "And you did that all for me?"

Lykke shrugged as she nodded. "I suppose."

"And if we get married, then we could choose to be merpeople or we could choose to be humans?" Emil asked.

"That's what the magic says," said Lykke.

They kissed again. But this time, as they did, Lykke felt … odd. As she drew back, she could see that Emil had a strange look too.

"Lykke, I don't want to—I mean, we can get married if you—it's just … kissing you is like kissing my sister," said Emil.

"It is!" cried Lykke. "I believed I loved you but—"

"You're my best friend," said Emil. "And, of course, you are beautiful, and brave, and you could not be dearer to me—"

"But we are not meant to be married," Lykke finished, firmly.

Emil looked worried. "But Lykke, if we do not marry, you have given up everything—forever—for nothing."

Lykke thought back over the weeks she had spent with Emil and all the amazing experiences she had had. "That's fine with me," she grinned. "I thought it was you I loved—but I think it's actually life on land! This has been the most wonderful adventure —and there's so much more to see!"

So, Lykke began her new life. Emil made her the head of his sailing fleet. "Nobody knows the oceans better than you," he said. "You can guide our ships through even the most dangerous of seas and at the end of every voyage will be a new land to explore."

Lykke soon became known as the best admiral any fleet had ever had. She knew the sea so well that the other sailors nicknamed her "The Mermaid." Whenever she heard this, she would catch Emil's eye and smile.

And if she ever did miss her family, she would wait until after the sun had set and tiptoe down to the beach. Silent as a seal, she would slip into the water and swim to meet them, but she would always return to the land and the life that she loved.

Guimara,
the Giant Princess

Adapted from *Tales of Giants from Brazil*, by Elsie Spicer Eells

Once, there was a princess giant, named Guimara. She lived with her father and mother, the king and queen of the giants, in their enormous palace in the realm of the giants. They were so tall that the king's head almost reached the clouds and Guimara wasn't much smaller.

The giant realm was very remote from all the human kingdoms of the world and separated from them by a huge wall. Guimara longed for fresh company and to hear new stories, for nobody had arrived at the palace in many long years and she had heard all of her parents' stories a thousand times.

One day, an adventurous human prince, called João, got lost when he was out hunting and stumbled into the Giant Realm. Guimara's father found him and was impressed by the prince's bravery, for João did not quiver before him. He invited João to live in his palace as a servant. Prince João thought living in the Realm of the Giants sounded like an excellent adventure, so he accepted the king's offer and moved into the enormous palace.

Princess Guimara was delighted to have a new companion. To begin with, she just enjoyed hearing all of Prince João's tales, but before too long, she fell in love with the little man and he fell in love with her too. They knew that they were from very different realms, but they swore to each other that their love would overcome everything.

When they told Guimara's parents, however, the king was displeased. Although he thought Prince João was a fine human, he thought he ought to have a giant for a son-in-law. So, he began to think of a plot to get João out of their hair.

The next day, he sent for the prince. "João, my little man," he boomed. "My other servants have told me you have been boasting that you could tear my palace down in a single night and then build it up again before the dawn."

João was confused. "I've never said any such thing, Your Majesty," he said, politely.

The king sniffed. "Pity," he said. "If you could do something like that, I would respect you much more. I might even welcome you as a son-in-law."

João went and told Guimara what her father had said.

Guimara giggled. "So that's the game my father wants to play, is it?" she said. "Well, João, don't worry. I have magical powers. I can help you do exactly that and surprise my father."

João was doubtful; he had never seen his beloved's magical powers. But that night, Guimara took his hand and led him outside. Using her magic, she tore down the whole palace.

Soon, it was just a pile of rubble, surrounding the king, queen, and all of their servants, who had all been asleep in bed. As they rubbed their eyes and sat up sleepily, Guimara ducked behind a clump of trees and directed her magic through João, so that it looked like he was putting the palace back together all by himself.

As dawn broke, João slid the last roof tile into place and turned to find himself face to face with the king. João bowed carefully, so as not to fall off the roof. "Exactly as it was before, Your Majesty," he said.

"Hmmm," replied the King, for he had seen João do it, but he was certain his daughter had been involved somehow. "But while you have been doing this, my other servants have been talking about you again. They say that you also boasted that it would take you only a single night to turn the Isle of Wild Beasts into a beautiful flower garden."

"I didn't say any such thing, Your Majesty," João insisted.

The Giant King raised an eyebrow and walked away.

Guimara crept out of her hiding place. "It will be great fun to turn the Isle of Wild Beasts into a lovely garden!" she cried.

That night, João and Guimara crept out and sailed over to the island. It was a land of gnarled trees, poisonous flowers, and many monsters, but Guimara had soon turned it into the most beautiful paradise. Guimara and João danced in the flower meadow until they noticed the sun starting to rise.

The king arrived as dawn broke, to see Prince João standing alone by an exquisite silver fountain in the middle of a perfect garden. Though she was hidden, the king was even more certain that his daughter had been involved and he was furious. "How dare you make a fool of me?!" he roared. "You will be sorry for this, João!"

All day, the giant king raged, destroying forests and mountains in his anger. Princess Guimara watched him from her bedroom window and worried for the safety of her little human prince. "João, I believe the time has come for us to leave," she said.

That night, Guimara crept out of her room. She ran to the stables, where João had saddled the best horse, which could travel one hundred leagues with every step. They mounted the horse together and rode away.

The next morning, the king awoke to find Guimara and João were gone, along with the best horse from his stables. "That human wretch!" he exclaimed. "What shall I do?"

"Calm yourself, my dear," said the queen. "Take the other horse that can go a hundred leagues in a step. If you go soon, you will catch up with them quite quickly."

"You are right, my dear," said the king. He did as she said.

Meanwhile, Guimara and João had grown tired and stopped for a rest. When Guimara heard fast hoofbeats approaching, she stood up and squinted. "It's my father!" she cried. "I must hide us, quickly!"

She used her magic to turn Prince João into an old man. She turned the horse into a tree, the saddle into a bed of onions, and the musket that they carried into a butterfly. Finally, she turned herself into a little river.

When the king arrived at the river, he was confused. He could have sworn he had seen his daughter and João sitting there moments before. He turned to the old man sitting by the river. "Old man, have you seen a small human man and a beautiful giant woman?"

The old man shook his head. "No, I have not. But I planted these onions. Aren't they magnificent?"

The giant looked at the bed of onions and wrinkled his nose. The smell was so strong that he didn't like to stay near them. As he edged away, a butterfly flew straight at his eyes. The Giant dodged away, flapping his hands. He looked all around him. There was no sign of Guimara and João. With a sigh, he went home.

This time, when he talked to the queen, she rolled her eyes and put her hands on her hips. "You silly giant! Surely you know our daughter's magic when you see it? She had changed herself into the river. I'm sure the tree was actually the horse, the onions were the saddle, and the butterfly was actually a musket. And I would bet my crown that the old man you spoke to was Prince João himself, disguised by Guimara's magic."

The king slammed his hand down on the table. "How dare they try to trick me again!"

"Well, you don't make it hard," his wife muttered. "I will come with you this time and they shall not find it so easy."

This time, the giant king and queen caught up with the lovers even more quickly. Guimara's mother saw through all Guimara's tricks. The edge of the Giant realm was in sight, but Guimara worried that they wouldn't reach it.

Just as her father reached out to grab her, Guimara used her final trick. She threw a handful of magic dust in her parents' eyes. Everything around them became so dark that they could not see. Guimara picked up João and scrambled over the wall into the human realm.

They raced away, through the forest, with João directing Guimara toward his own palace. Once they were far into the human realm, and certain that the giant king and queen were not following, they paused to catch their breath.

"And now we must find somewhere to live," Prince João said. "My palace is large for a human building, but I am afraid you will not fit in, my love."

Guimara thought hard. She wanted to be with her beloved and she knew that using her magical powers, she could make herself human-sized. But she didn't want to change everything about herself. "Your palace is large for humans, you say?"

"Indeed. Far bigger than any human would need," said João.

"Then why don't we both be large humans?" Guimara said, with a twinkle in her eye.

She used her magical powers to make herself a bit smaller, and to make João a bit bigger so that they met in the middle. "There! Now we shall fit your palace and we're the same size!" said Guimara, with a grin.

So, thanks to Guimara's quick thinking and magic, the two lovers were free to start their new life in the human realm. They were different from everyone else, but they didn't mind because they had each other.

The Maiden and the Falcon

Adapted from *The Feather of Finist the Falcon* by Alexander Afanasyev

There once was a young girl called Alyonushka. She lived in Russia, a very long time ago, with her father and her two sisters. They were not a rich family. Their father worked hard to make sure that they always had enough food to eat, but there was never much money left over for anything else.

One day, their father was going to work at the local fair. He hoped to do good business, perhaps even enough to get the girls a treat. He asked each of them what they would like. Zia, the eldest sister, asked for a new dress. Dinara, the middle sister, asked for a pretty shawl. Alyonushka thought carefully. What she really wanted was a way to escape their life of poverty altogether … and she thought she knew how.

"Father, I would like a feather from Finist the Falcon."

Her father frowned. He had heard of the huge falcon, who could often be seen swooping over the forests and fields, but he had no idea why his daughter wanted a feather from that famous bird.

Zia and Dinara laughed at her, but Alyonushka smiled to herself, for she knew something that they didn't. She had heard that Finist the Falcon was in actual fact a prince from the next kingdom, who could change shape at will. She hoped that he might be able to help her fly away from their small village and start a new life.

At the fair, the merchant sold many of his wares. He bought a beautiful dress for Zia and a very fine shawl for Dinara. Then, he saw the falcon swooping through the sky above him. The merchant followed the bird for a long time, and eventually, when it landed for a rest, the merchant sneaked up and plucked a feather from its tail.

All three of the girls were delighted with their gifts. The older two twirled around the house in their new clothes. Alyonushka took the feather up to her bedroom and left it on the windowsill. She hoped that as Finist flew above the house, he would notice his feather and come back to collect it.

That night, Finist flew in through Alyonushka's window and changed into his human form. Alyonushka's breath was taken away and she forgot all about what she was going to ask him; all she wanted to do was spend time with him.

Finist returned the next night and the night after that. Finist even promised to teach her how to fly, like him. They talked and talked and fell deeply in love with one another.

"My darling, if ever I don't return one night, come looking for me." Finist would tell her. "You will wear out three pairs of iron boots and then you will find me."

Alyonushka promised she would.

Alyonushka kept Finist a secret from her sisters. She knew that if they were to find out about him, they would try to break them up out of jealousy. When Finist brought her fine gifts, she hid them under her bed.

But her sisters grew suspicious all the same. They noticed how mysteriously happy Alyonushka was, as well as how tired she seemed. When they tried to sneak into her room at night to see what was going on, they found the door locked and heard the sound of a man's voice inside.

"Father, Alyonushka has a boyfriend that she is sneaking in at night," they told the merchant.

He laughed. "Don't be silly, girls, what a ridiculous tale."

But Zia and Dinara didn't give up. They slipped into the bedroom during the day and discovered the gifts beneath the bed.

"He must be climbing in the window," said Zia.

"Let's attach knives to the frame," said Dinara. "If we hear a man shout with pain tonight, we will know."

The two sisters secretly did just that and waited for night to fall. As Alyonushka was going to her room, they distracted her.

Finist arrived and was stabbed by the knives. Alyonushka was not there and he believed he had been betrayed. He ran away, bleeding, into the night.

When Alyonushka eventually got into her room, she found the bloodied knives and saw what her sisters had done.

"How dare you?" she said, furiously. "You drove my love away just because you don't have one. You are no longer my sisters."

Alyonushka waited several nights for Finist to come back, but he didn't. She knew she had to do what he had always told her. She went to the village and swapped her own winter boots for a pair of heavy iron shoes. Then, she set out on her journey, walking in the direction Finist had always flown from.

It was hard to walk in the shoes. Alyonushka's feet dragged and she was panting after only

a few steps. But she knew she had to find Finist and tell him the truth about what had really happened.

She walked miles and miles and miles, into a dark, enchanted forest. She saw with surprise that the iron boots were becoming rusty. Just as her first pair of shoes wore out, she spied the hut of a wise woodland witch, called a Baba Yaga. You could tell a Baba Yaga's hut because they had legs like giant chickens and moved noisily around the forest. As Alyonushka approached, the Baba Yaga opened her door and welcomed her in.

"My dear child, where do you go and what can I help you with?" asked the kindly Baba Yaga.

Alyonushka told her of her mission.

"You are indeed going the right way," the Baba Yaga said. "But you still have a long way to go."

She fed Alyonushka, gave her a new pair of iron shoes and a silver spinning wheel, and sent her on her way.

Alyonushka walked on and on, up thickly wooded mountains, and past sparkling lakes, until she came to another Baba Yaga's hut. This Baba Yaga also told her she was going in the right direction. Then, the witch fed her some delicious soup, gave her some new shoes and a golden egg, and sent her on her way.

Alyonushka walked farther still, through shaded valleys and across sun-dappled glades, until she wore out her third pair of shoes as she finally reached the edge of the forest. There was one more Baba Yaga's hut sitting at the of the trees.

This Baba Yaga told Alyonushka she was almost there.

"See, there is the palace of Prince Finist, yonder. But you must hurry. The word is that he is set to marry a princess tomorrow. There's going to be a grand ball to celebrate, and everyone's invited."

The Baba Yaga pressed a magical needle that could sew by itself into Alyonushka's hands and sent her on her way.

When Alyonushka arrived at the palace, she asked to see Prince Finist. She was told that he was out hunting and would be back later. Alyonushka planned to wait for him, but word reached the ears of the princess that a beautiful girl was asking to see Finist.

She went and found Alyonushka. "What do you want with my husband-to-be?"

Alyonushka decided to be truthful and told the princess the whole story.

The princess crossed her arms. "So, you are here to steal him away from me? Hah, I will not let you near him."

Alyonushka hung her head. "I never got to say goodbye, and he must think that I betrayed him. Please may I see him tonight? I wish to just say farewell and let him know that I was not the one who hurt him. I can give you gifts." She held out all the precious items the Baba Yagas had given to her.

"Fine," said the princess. "Wait in that room and I'll call you when it's time." She took the magical objects and walked away, laughing to herself. The princess went to see the old magic woman who lived in the palace and asked for a way to make Finist fall into a sleep so deep he could not be woken until she wished it. That way, the pesky Alyonushka couldn't take her prince away from her.

The old woman gave the princess a magic pin. "Put this in your prince's hair. He will sleep until it is removed."

The princess waited for Finist to return from his flight. Once he did, she told him to rest on a comfy couch. Then, she slipped the pin into his hair and he fell fast asleep.

The princess showed Alyonushka to the room. "He's all yours until dawn," she laughed, cruelly.

Poor Alyonushka couldn't understand why Finist didn't wake up. She tried again and again to wake him.

"This is an enchanted sleep," she gasped eventually. "The princess has tricked me!"

She stroked Finist's hair tenderly, remembering the long nights they had spent in conversation. As she stroked, the pin fell out of his hair and Finist sprang awake.

"Alyonushka? What are you doing here?" he exclaimed.

Alyonushka explained everything—what her sisters had done, the endless miles she had walked, and finally how she had bought one more night with him from the princess. When she finished, Finist looked angered.

"She sold me for some magical objects? While you, dear Alyonushka, journeyed all this way to find me. I know what true love looks like. Please, will you marry me?"

"Of course!" Alyonushka cried.

So, there was a wedding the next day but it was not the one Finist's kingdom had been expecting.

After they were married, they lived happily ever after—and in time Alyonushka learned to fly as a falcon too. They would soar through the sky together, and each time they passed over the hut of a Baba Yaga, Alyonushka called down her thanks.

Céline,
Kitchen Queen

Adapted from Donkeyskin by Charles Perrault

A long time ago in France, there lived a girl called Céline. She loved to bake cakes and after many years of hard work, she finally got her dream job working in the palace kitchens of the King and Queen.

Not far from the kitchens were the palace stables, where there lived a magic donkey. This creature was famous all over the kingdom, because it could turn things into gold. Céline became fond of the donkey, and whenever she took a break from her kitchen duties, she would visit the creature to pet it.

Not long after Céline started working at the palace, the Queen died. The whole kingdom mourned, for the Queen had been very popular. More popular than her husband, in fact.

After the Queen's death, something inside the King broke. He became bitter, cruel, and spiteful. After several months, he decided that he would marry again. His new wife, he declared, would be an improvement on the old one in every way. She would be more beautiful, more talented, and more beloved by the people.

One day, as the King was wandering around the palace, he ended up in the kitchens. He caught sight of Céline. Even in a dirty apron, with messy, tousled hair and flour on her nose, the king could see that Céline was beautiful. He decided that she was the woman he wanted to marry.

Céline was horrified when the king proposed to her. But she also knew that if she said no to the king, he might sack her.

She asked if she could think about his proposal overnight and the king agreed. Céline couldn't sleep as she tried to decide what to do. She stayed in the kitchen, pacing up and down. She tried to bake a cake to calm her nerves, but it didn't work. She paced some more. Then she baked some cookies to clear her mind. That didn't work either. Just as she was whipping up a batch of meringues, there was a loud POP and her fairy godmother appeared in the kitchen.

"Something on your mind, Céline?" asked Fairy Godmother, raising an eyebrow. She knew her goddaughter very well indeed and she knew that she baked through the night when she was worried.

Céline explained what had happened. "Please, Fairy Godmother, what do I do? I cannot marry him."

Fairy Godmother smiled. "Do not worry, my dear. The answer is simple. Say that you will marry him, but only on the condition that he gives you these things—a dress as bright as the sun, another dress that shines like the moon, and a dress that changes like a sunset."

"It's impossible to have dresses like that," Céline said, confused. "Nothing on earth is as bright as the sun, for a start."

"Exactly!" said Fairy Godmother. "He won't be able to give you any of those things and so you will be able to say that you can't marry him.

The next morning, Céline went to the king and told him her demands.

The King frowned for a moment—but then he smiled, his lips curling into a grimace that frightened Céline. "Done. And I will do one better, to prove my love for you. I will destroy my most valuable possession."

That evening, when Céline went back to her bedroom, three amazing dresses were waiting for her. One was as bright as the sun, another shone like the moon, and the third changed like a sunset. And next to the dresses lay the skin of the magic donkey.

"Oh no, poor donkey," Céline cried to herself. She dashed straight back down to the kitchen to try to think.

This time when Fairy Godmother appeared, Céline was surrounded by chocolate cupcakes and towers of cookies.

"Your plan didn't work," Céline gasped as she beat a bowl of eggs. "Now I have to marry him!"

"Calm yourself," Fairy Godmother said. "All is not lost. That magic donkey skin will make a great disguise. Go back to your room, then put it on and flee the palace."

"But my cakes! My job!" Céline wailed.

"There are other places to bake in this world," Fairy Godmother said, firmly. "And I will make sure we find you one of them."

So, Céline crept back to her room, put on the donkey skin, packed the fine dresses in a bag, and slipped out of the palace. She ran as far away as she could, looking like an old beggar woman. Eventually, she came to a new kingdom. She headed toward the royal palace. There were no jobs available in the main kitchen, but the royal farm in the palace grounds needed a cook.

"Although you'll have to clean yourself up a bit," said the farmer, wrinkling his nose at the smelly donkey skin.

Céline worked hard and impressed all the farmhands with the delicious cakes she made. She was wary of showing anyone her beauty, so she stayed disguised in the donkey skin as much as possible.

One day, the cook in the main palace kingdom was taken ill. All the servants were very worried, for it was the prince's birthday and they hadn't got a birthday cake for him! They sent word around the palace grounds that anyone who could bake should report to the main kitchen. The farmhands all said. "Why, Donkeyskin Girl can bake lovely cakes! Choose her!"

The head servant of the palace wrinkled his nose when he saw Céline. "But she is so ugly and dirty. She surely can't bake anything delicious!"

"Her cakes are the very best," said the farmhands, firmly.

So, Céline was taken up to the huge

palace kitchen. It was even grander than the kitchen at her last palace. Céline was thrilled and vowed to bake the greatest cake she had ever made.

The cake was enormous! There was a layer of every kind: chocolate, vanilla, coffee, toffee, strawberry, lemon, orange, and dozens more. It was decorated with hundreds of swirls of frosting, like a beautiful rainbow.

The head servant wouldn't let Céline carry it into the room in her smelly donkey skin, so she stood at the door, peeking in. All of the courtiers gasped and clapped as the beautiful cake was set before the prince.

The prince cut slices for everyone.

"This is the most delicious cake I have ever eaten in my entire life!" the prince cried.

Céline was so proud she couldn't help but do a little happy dance outside the door. But then the prince frowned, chewing slowly. He reached into his mouth and pulled out a silver ring.

Céline looked down and saw, with horror, that her silver ring was missing from her finger! She had baked it into the cake by mistake! She put her head in her hands, believing that she had ruined her chances of cooking in the palace kitchens.

"I will only marry the woman whose finger fits this ring," the prince announced. "For she was the one who made me this perfect cake."

Many of the ladies of the court immediately tried to pretend that they had baked the cake. But the ring didn't fit any of them. Several servants barged in and tried to take credit, but the ring didn't fit them either.

Céline wasn't sure that she wanted to tell the prince that she was the baker. She just wanted to bake, not find a husband! But before she could slip away, the head servant grabbed her hand and pulled her into the middle of the room.

"Your highness, this—er—lady is the one who baked your cake."

Everyone turned to stare at Céline. She saw all the rich people of the court sneering at her floury hands and the donkey skin that she wore.

But when she looked at the prince, he looked enchanted. He held out the ring. "Is this yours?"

Céline reluctantly held out her hand and the prince slipped the ring onto her finger. It fit perfectly.

The prince smiled at her. "In that case, will you marry me?"

Céline gestured to her donkey skin. "Your highness, I am a humble servant wearing dirty fur robes. I am not suitable for a prince to marry."

The prince waved a hand. "What you are wearing is just an outside thing, and being a servant is a perfectly fine job. I don't care about those. Anyone who can bake cakes full of love like that is the most beautiful person on the inside and that's someone who I would like to marry."

Céline felt touched by the prince's kind words. "Your highness, you are very kind. I do not feel ready to marry anyone. But if you think so highly of me, I wonder if I could ask you something?"

"Anything!" said the prince.

"Please may I have a job in your palace kitchen?" Céline asked. "All I really want to do is bake cakes."

"Done!" declared the prince.

Thrilled, Céline shed the donkey skin at last and all the courtiers were surprised by how beautiful and young she was.

From that day on, Céline made every cake in the palace kitchens and her baking was legendary throughout the kingdom. The prince would come down to visit her—and taste her cakes—every day and eventually, after many years of dating, he asked her once again to marry him.

Céline agreed, but on one condition—that she never had to stop baking!

Princess Kaguya's
Great Adventure

Adapted from *The Tale of the Bamboo Cutter*, a tenth-century Japanese story

There once was a princess called Kaguya. She was no ordinary princess, for she lived in the great kingdom of Celestia, on the moon. Celestia was full of magic and delightful things, but Kaguya was meant to stay in her room in the palace, studying. Her parents, the king and queen, told her that being a princess was a serious business. She needed to learn all of the Lunar Laws and the history of her people by the time she was grown up, so that she could be the best queen possible.

Kaguya tried her best to concentrate on her moon books, but she usually ended up gazing out of the window at the Earth. The swirling globe of green and blue was beautiful and mysterious to her. She wondered what it would be like to live down there.

One night, she grew tired of just looking and wondering.

I want to see it all for myself. I want to be a human on Earth.

It would be an adventure, away from her books and studying. Kaguya knew her parents wouldn't approve, so she waited until they were distracted by a visit from the Starry Ambassador and then she slipped out of her room. She tiptoed down the golden staircase and outside. The golden light of the moon was beaming down toward the earth. Kaguya knew a bit of magic, so she flew down to Earth on a moonbeam. She landed in the middle of a bamboo forest in Japan.

Kaguya didn't know how human babies were born, since children were born differently on Celestia. So, she planted herself in the ground and waited to start her new human life.

A little while later, an old, childless bamboo cutter called Taketori no Okina was walking past. He noticed a stalk of bamboo that was glowing with a golden light. Curious as to what was causing the bamboo to glow, he cut the stalk open to find a baby the size of his thumb. It was Princess Kaguya. Taketori no Okina was delighted to find such a lovely little girl and took her home to his wife.

As Kaguya grew, she caught up with normal human children in size. Although she never told her Earth parents where she was really from, she loved them dearly and did her best to be a good daughter. She had great fun exploring everything that she was allowed to, such as her local town and the bamboo forest, but even on Earth, Kaguya found that she was not free to go wherever she pleased. She was always careful to keep her head down, as well. She was sure her parents would be looking for her from the Moon and she didn't want them to spot her.

Years passed and Kaguya grew up to be a very beautiful woman. She was famous throughout the land. Lots and lots of young men came to the house, asking if they could marry Kaguya.

Kaguya was not interested in marrying anyone. From what she could see, getting married to someone would just mean that someone else would be around to tell her where she could and couldn't go. But when five princes arrived, each asking for her hand in marriage, Taketori no Okina begged Kaguya to at least consider them. He worried that the princes would be angry at being rejected straight away.

"Very well, Father," Kaguya said, with a twinkle in her eye. "I'll give them all a chance."

She met the princes and told each of them to bring her an item that she knew was impossible to find. She told the first prince to bring her the legendary begging bowl of Shakyamuni.

The prince could not find such a bowl, so he bought an expensive stone bowl and presented it to her.

"This bowl does not glow with holy light; it is a fake!" Kaguya exclaimed. "I might have married you if you were honest." She sent the prince away.

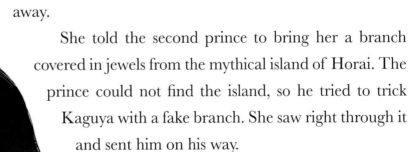

She told the second prince to bring her a branch covered in jewels from the mythical island of Horai. The prince could not find the island, so he tried to trick Kaguya with a fake branch. She saw right through it and sent him on his way.

The third prince, she asked to bring her the legendary robe of the fire rat.

The prince didn't want

to go anywhere near a fire rat, so he gave her a robe he had bought from a merchant. Kaguya laughed and told him to leave.

The fourth prince was told to bring her a jewel from a dragon's neck. He tried hard but was forced to turn back from his journey to the dragon's lair because of a most terrible storm.

"Let's take it as a sign that it wasn't meant to be," said Kaguya, with a grin, as he left.

She asked the fifth prince to bring her a cowry shell laid by a swallow. The prince could find no such thing anywhere and returned to the palace in a rage.

"I wouldn't marry such a grump anyway!" Kaguya said.

She and Taketori no Okina laughed together over how she had tricked the princes.

But the next man who knocked on the door was very different to all the princes who had come before. It was Mikado, the Emperor of Japan. When Kaguya opened the door, Mikado was struck by her amazing beauty and the way she seemed to glow from the inside.

"Are you Kaguya?" Mikado asked.

Kaguya dipped her head. She knew who Mikado was and she didn't want to be rude. "I am."

"Ah, the cruel lady herself. I hear you send suitors on impossible missions so that you may laugh at them when they fail."

Kaguya's eyes danced. "Perhaps ...."

Mikado grinned back. "How interesting. Might I ask why?"

"Because I don't want to be married," Kaguya told him. "I would rather go on adventures, not stay at home with a husband."

Mikado looked thoughtful. "Is that so? You know, I don't really want to get married either. But emperors are supposed to, you know. In fact," he chuckled, "that's actually why I came. I thought perhaps I could pretend to my advisors that you turned me down so I don't have to get married."

Kaguya suddenly had a wonderful idea. "Why don't we go exploring together? People will think you are trying to woo me and neither of us will have to bother with any suitors for a while."

"That's a great idea!" said Mikado. "Where would you like to go?"

"Everywhere!" cried Kaguya.

The journey was everything Kaguya could have hoped for. She was finally able to visit all the places she had seen from the moon—the huge cities, the great rivers, the forests, and finally, the mountains.

Mount Fuji was the tallest mountain in the empire. As they stood at the top, Kaguya gazed at Earth spread out beneath her, while Mikado looked up at the moon.

"We are so much closer to the moon up here," he said. "I can see every bump on it!" Suddenly, he yelped in alarm. "Who's that? What's happening?"

Kaguya turned to see her parents and several guards from Celestia riding down toward them on a moonbeam.

Kaguya knew that they must have spotted her because she had climbed so high. She quickly turned to Mikado and told him the whole story.

Mikado's jaw dropped. "You're from the moon?"

Kaguya's parents stepped off the moonbeam, looking furious.

"Kaguya, it is time to go home," said her mother, sternly. "We've all been extremely worried."

"You belong in Celestia," added her father.

Although she was sad, Kaguya knew that they were right.

"At least I got to see everything, thanks to you," she said to Mikado. "But let us stay friends. I will write to you and send letters down on a moonbeam."

"But how will I write to you?" Mikado asked.

"Bring your letters up here and burn them," said Kaguya. "The smoke will rise all the way up to the Moon and I will know what your letters say."

She stepped onto the moonbeam and floated back up through the sky, waving goodbye to her friend.

Kaguya and Mikado wrote to each other all the time. Everyone in the empire got used to all the smoke at the top of Mount Fuji as the Emperor and his best friend stayed in touch.

Kaguya knew her place was on the moon, and she loved her home, but her heart always held a special place for her greatest adventure, visiting Earth.